DAVID RICH

twelve stories

. . . .

Twelve Stories

©2017 David Rich

ISBN: 978-1-9402-4485-3

designed and produced by
Indie Author Warehouse
12 High Street, Thomaston, Maine
www.indieauthorwarehouse.com

Printed in the United States of America

ACKNOWLEDGMENTS

My first acknowledgment goes, not to a person, but to a brick-and-mortar institution, the Harvard Institute for Learning in Retirement. Here a group of five hundred fifty retired persons with a myriad of interests carry on the happy task of peer-led late-life learning. Here I had my first chance to write something other than a contract.

Prior to my retirement I was an attorney at Sheraton Hotels Corporation headquarters in Boston. As such, my writing generally was of a legal nature with its many parentheticals and convolutions, full of appurtenances and whereas, now therefores.

For a long time, though, I had cherished the notion that there was a lively verbal imagination swimming beneath the surface crust of these legalisms, which wasn't able to break through that crust until I retired.

In 2000 at HILR, I signed up for a poetry group that was led by the wonderful Fran Vaughan, a gifted poet and an inspirational teacher.

I liked poetry fine but wanted to try fiction. Again, HILR was ready for me with a course led by Paul Pemsler. The two years with Paul and talented classmates clarified for me that short fiction was what I wanted to write.

Outside the classroom, I have been a member of several different writing groups, chiefly comprised of HILR members. Each of the groups has provided the invaluable opportunity to read and be read critically and the needed prodding to continue writing when the spirit flagged.

Thanks to Boston Writers Publishing & Cooperative, who handled professionally the many tasks required to get the stories into print.

Finally, special thanks goes to my wonderful family: Ellen, Catherine, and Matthew. Matt designed the marvelous cover. Ellen, throughout the lengthy process of composition, commented perceptively on the stories and helped me get beyond many stalled moments.

CONTENTS

• • • • • • • • • • • •

twelve stories

FINAL APPROACH TO NIRVANA

Ladies and gentlemen, this is your bored-out-of-his-mind captain speaking. Welcome to Flight number, ah…what's the number…well, I'm pretty sure it's Flight Forty-Three. Let me check. Yes, it's Forty-Three…Delta's mediocre service…Hong Kong to New Delhi…flying time today will be five hours and seventy-six minutes…hah…a little brain teaser for you there…should be arriving about seven-fifteen in the morning…maybe later…maybe earlier…maybe never…weather currently hazy and polluted, just like always…temperature a brain-frying forty degrees centigrade…if I can be of assistance…blah, blah, blah, blah. Enough of that crap.

Well, we just took off and the wheels are up. I'm finally on my way to India. Gautama Buddha, here I come! I'm in the wheel bay of a Boeing 747, all by myself. When I shine the flashlight around, my fellow passengers are these mega-sized tires, squatting next to me, making big, dark shadows on the walls.

I have authenticated my presence here by scratching my name on the wall and today's date, which as far as I'm concerned is Buddha's birthday. You can find scholars who claim every day in the year as his birthday, so my pick is as good as anyone's. Anyway, this trip, courtesy of the Delta first class frigid wheel bay, is going to be a new birth for me.

Let's get the technical questions out of the way quickly, because I need to meditate with the cold that's coming. First, my voice is being recorded on one of those notorious "black boxes." Buddha loves a good paradox, so for our first paradox of the flight, it's actually orange in color, though it does just what the box up in the cockpit does. Records the conversation of those who have our lives in their hands—the sighs and swears and boredom; the copilot's fantasies about Mary, the new attendant in economy with a first-class body. If there's a problem it'll tell you who screwed up. And I have this noise-minimizing device that will make my recording pretty clear, even in this wind tunnel. So we're going to know what happens to yours truly. Okay on that one?

Second, I've got oxygen—a real system, a diluter-demand oxygen system that is good up to 40,000 feet. So I've got air. Third, I've figured out the outside temperature and wind factor at 38,000 feet. It's like –80°F. Pretty cold, huh? If the meditation program and my generally elevated temperature don't work, I've hedged my bets. I got myself encased in several layers of some of the finest Arctic wear available, which disappeared mysteriously from a Hong Kong Army-Navy store the other day. I am not suicidal.

How I got on the plane is the next question, right? Just let me say that my presence is the result of careful planning, precision execution, and some security lapses I will be happy to point out to the proper authorities if I have the chance. Getting into the wheel bay has been done a lot before. If you go online you can find that men, and even young, innocent boys, have managed this business—stowing away, that is. Unfortunately, they didn't survive. They evaded the lax security but hadn't done any survival planning.

Why did the others do it? Mostly, because they were desperate to get out of Africa or some other benighted place and have a better life. A perfectly reasonable, if fatal, desire. Au contraire, there is one story about two Frenchmen wearing red Air France outfits who hid out on a Paris–Beijing flight. They froze and fell out when the wheel bay opened and in the form of icy projectiles crashed through the roof of a flimsy siheyuan in downtown Beijing, enlivening the existence of some flabbergasted Chinese peasants hunched over their rice bowls. The men were leaving Paris for a dicier place. What goes? Whatever the rationale, we'll never know.

And why am I doing this crazy-seeming thing? Am I nuts like those Frenchmen? Maybe. A show-off; a spotlight grabber? You name it! Anyway I'm Larry Hilt. The second youngest of five brothers, all bigger than me, even the kid who was born when I was four. Forty-five years old now. No children. No job. Three wives. None now. I tried really hard in my own way, I think, but I just couldn't seem to settle down. Always felt I was running a temperature above normal. Feverish. From the time I was twenty-two until I was forty, I lived in Hollywood and did stunts for movies. Back before computers took all the fun out of it. I was, you know, one of those guys who stepped in for the big star, when the fists and chairs started flying around the bar; or when he jumped off a cliff into shark-infested waters. One of those guys who took the risks and the bumps and didn't really get any credit. I'll bet my temperature was like 100 before almost any stunt, like I think it is right now.

Anyway, the stunt life was plenty tough, but I really loved it. I survived because I was pretty good at figuring out the risks and the odds and how to deal with them. If you didn't do that you were dead.

I had to quit five years ago. After surviving terrible floods, whipped up by Hollywood wind machines, and chases up and down steep, rocky canyons on frothing stallions, I fell down a long flight of stairs trying to elude my third wife, who was after me with a sharp implement, and broke my leg in three places. It was goodbye to the stunt world and hello to a new world that I couldn't cope with. Of course, I wasn't really coping so well before, but I was so busy that I didn't notice.

When I was growing up with all those bigger brothers around I had to work extra hard to get any attention from anybody, particularly my parents, who were always busy fighting and hardly noticed anybody else anyway. They threw things at each other a lot, and we got pretty good at ducking. I started to do stunts when I was young:

"Hey, look at me way up in this tree. Yeah, yeah, way up here! Can you see me?"

I was a very nimble climber but the best I ever got from my father was, "Come down, you stupid twerp!" using less gracious language. When I got a little older, though, the girls paid attention and giggled and shrieked when I did that or things like grabbing hold of a water moccasin and dancing it around. Mighty cute, that, huh!

That's all highly interesting and informative, you say. But what of Buddha? You said, did you not, at the outset with some spirit, 'Gautama Buddha, here I come'? You're right! I'm glad you're paying attention. Here's the story:

when my last wife walked out, she left me with a leg broken in three places and my spirits and my heart shattered far worse. With my stunting days and marriages over, I went from Hollywood's bright lights and sizzle back to my humble roots: that humble log cabin near an alligator-infested swamp. Ah, forget I said that. Buddha wants only right and true speech.

Washed up down south, back home in New Orleans near where I was born. Took a job as a waiter and did pretty well after my leg healed. I did a trick where I would run and slide across the floor on my knees with a bunch of loaded trays, never spilling a thing. I'd do other charming routines like that as well. The business on the knees hurt a lot, but I did it anyway. Took up with a number of different women, but the length of each relationship got shorter and shorter until they were lasting one night. Maybe half a night. Okay, an hour. I had been hot-blooded and crazy for sex since I was fifteen and lay with Ruby Ann on a moist, mossy piece of earth just outside of town. She raised me to heaven by her innocent, perfect body and what she let me do. But the sex stuff wasn't doing the trick. All the time while I was getting more and restless, I really was desperate for something steady.

Point of order. Since I'm into truth-telling here, I believe I said I was forty-five. Actually I'm closer to fifty. Anyway, one evening I was out wandering around and went by a small store with the door open. I heard some chanting, listened for a minute, and went inside. There were maybe twenty people inside seated cross-legged on cushions or on chairs. All around on the walls were these green and red gods and goddesses and, then, there was a figure, Buddha himself, sitting golden and steady on a small pedestal. A fellow named Herman was giving instruction for first-time meditators, so I took a chair and listened. Herman was talking about giving your mind a break, letting your thoughts flow through, and not beating up on yourself. Then, near the end of the session, he told the story of Buddha's enlightenment, which intrigued me. I left the Meditation Center, feeling I might really be able to change my chaotic life.

The second time I went, Herman talked about desire as the root of suffering. All my desire was ruining me. Making me hotter and hotter and more and more unhappy. So I started meditating and have meditated a lot over a three-year period. It's helped me. But I wasn't getting what I felt I needed.

Sometime after I started "the practice," as they call it, I read about Tibetan monks who were so good at meditation that they could sit outdoors in subzero temperatures on blocks of ice, wearing next to nothing. Sometimes they could even get the ice to melt! Honest to Buddha! Seriously, something about those Tibetan monks sitting on their ice block, without their asses and balls becoming numb and falling off, got to the stuntman in me. I tried some meditation in just my Hanes briefs, and the ice didn't melt, but I could keep at it for a while and my scrotum didn't try to ascend north into my body for warmth. And I didn't head for the bar of an evening so much.

This dramatic approach got me thinking and since I have this big tendency to be impatient, I began to think of finding a quicker way to enlightenment. I'm not saying there are really shortcuts. But I wanted to find a way to jump-start my progress. Plus I feel time's winged chariot drawing near, as the poet said in a different context. So obviously this is what was needed: a change of venue, India; a unique form of transportation, the wheel bay calling on my well-honed skills as a stuntman and survivor; and a chance to pit my hot blood against the frigidity of the remote world at 38,000 feet. I figure I can survive this trip. If I don't…well, we tried not to think about that back in the old days when we jumped off those cliffs.

Okay, stop talking. It's time to meditate.

Hello, again. I'm back. Even though you're not supposed to judge, I'm going to say the meditation went well. Now, with your indulgence and because I think it's a good survival technique for me, I'm going to talk a little about Buddha's enlightenment. Well, the part of it that affects me most directly.

It's pretty well known that Buddha first tried every austerity, starving himself until he was thin as a rail; wandering in the forest, all hairy, ragged, and unwashed; begging till blue in the face. None of that over-the-top stuff worked.

So, Buddha went moderate and finally got enlightened by sitting motionless for a whole week under a Bodhi tree, a strange, squat, bare kind of a tree in a hot, dusty, dry, inhospitable town now called Sarnath in India. He confronted Mara. Mara's the demon whose job it is to deny enlightenment by a combination of scare tactics and the dangling of delicious temptations in front of the seeker.

We'll skip the scare tactics, creatures with huge tongues covered with sharp ridges like a cheese grater and the mighty winds that bent the Bodhi tree to the ground. Buddha sat there and brushed those off.

What I want to get to was Mara's final and best shot. He unleashed a bevy of luscious, beautiful maidens scantily attired, carrying heavy, juicy melons, and these maidens danced around Buddha and dangled those ripe fruits in front of him. When he didn't go for the tempting tidbits, the maidens took off the last of their gauzy garments and tried to roll their own voluptuous fruits all over him. Buddha's defenses got a little porous for a minute there. A close observer might have seen Buddha twitch, maybe once or twice, and his eyes rotate, but he kept the heat turned down. That was it. Buddha got enlightened and Mara got vanquished.

Okay, I'd better try a little meditative vanquishing of my own. I can report it is fiercely cold here and body temperature is down. Like what? 95°F means mild hypothermia; at 91°F amnesia comes along; 82°F, you lose consciousness. Let's say right now I'm hovering at 93°F. I read that that was a seven-year-old girl in Sweden who survived an all time of low of 56.7°F. She's my hero.

I'm back. I'm sorry to say I can't be as affable and full of charm as I have been. I'm keeping my right hand, in my nice double-fur-lined mitten, on the bottom of the plane, the closest thing to earth around here, to stay grounded like Buddha did. Oops, I just slid around a little bit. The aircraft is experiencing some turbulence, as they say. They're telling them upstairs to stay in their seats and keep their seatbelts loosely fastened. They'd be more honest if they'd tell them they can't get up and take a piss no matter what. Come on, Larry, stop with that stuff.

I just pulled up my mask for a second and turned on the flashlight. I can see great clouds of breath sailing around me. Is this my spirit turning into substance or something like that? It's supposed to be the other way around. Herman, back at the Center, used to say, "Follow your breath. That's the key to meditation." I'll send him a postcard when I get to India and tell him how it works at 38,000 feet.

I'd like to be at the Center right now. The Center was nice and warm and bright, and it's unbelievably cold and dark here, but this is my center right now. I had to move on. See you.

Back. That was a long time, I think. Little dazed now. Body slowing down. Yeah, slowed down so much I can't really feel where I begin and end. I think I'm talking funny, too. I can't tell whether it's really hot or really cold. Can you believe that? Anyway I do know I'm still alive. I'm thinking and what was good enough for Descartes is good enough for me right now.

I'm back once more. Hope it's not the last time. Cold is searing. Wind howling. Tearing at me a million miles an hour. Noise is deafening, even with earpieces. Not feeling as cocky now as I think I sounded earlier. Even those bare-assed Tibetans would be challenged plenty here. Except that maybe is what is helping to keep me alive. Lost track of time. Time check. Two hours left. Elements crawling all over me like Mara's minions, but not sexy. Cold. Cold. Cold.

Something pretty strange just happened. Feeling warmer. Easier to talk. I got a little frozen crazy and had a sort of a vision of a lot of the women I've been with in my lifetime, including the wives. Quite a crowd.

Anyway, they were all there, all older and they didn't look their American or whatever selves. They were all wearing some kind of bright colored saris and they were all darker-skinned and had long black hair and sloe eyes with kohl, or whatever they call it, dabbed around the eyes. And they were all dancing. Not doing zydeco or anything like that but swaying back and forth making these movements with their arms and legs, and each of them seemed to have several arms and legs waving around, you know, like statues of Shiva's consorts. Sometimes they would shake their heads back and forth like Indians do, when they look like they are saying yes but mean no. Or, maybe, it's vice versa. So there they were. All Indian now, whatever that means.

Anyway bless them all, these undulating women, because they kept me going. They were still full of a lovely, sensual ripeness, still highly desirable and generating heat when I needed heat. But here's another thing: They looked sadder, wiser, like they had lived a little and it hadn't all been easy. I hadn't been easy. As I looked at them, I felt more kindly than I had in the past. Then, I had a funny sense of coolness blowing through the scene. I don't mean cold. I mean like an afternoon breeze making a hot afternoon suddenly pleasant. This heat and cool stuff wasn't real of course. It was part of the dream.

Okay, time out is over. Here comes the cold again. I think this may be the last round.

So I've been gone for a long time. Maybe a short time. I don't know. It got really frigid again. But now I feel—no, I know—that the plane is coming down. It's getting warmer. Yeah, if you can call 20- below warmer. Pretty soon there's going to be the wildest noise, but there'll be light finally because the wheel bay is going to grind open and that badass, mighty Mara, wind will be whipping around here, trying to blow me out.

But here's the bit I've been saving for the last, if you're still with me. Where the stuntman may trump the meditator. I didn't tell you about it before. I got this parachute, so that when the doors open and the wind tries to rip me out, I'm on my way down. Not like those Frenchmen who scared the hell out of the poor Chinese when they ended up in their soup. I'm in control. Well, pretty much. I did this a lot in World War II movies. You remember, screaming, "Geronimo!" on the way down. Hey, he was an Indian too, right!

I am going to drift down slow and easy and steer myself into a nice, soft, pungent field with a lot of sacred cows staring at me. When I hit the ground I'll bury that parachute deep, deep down in a hole like it was my past life and thread my way through the piles of sacred dung with their crowns of worshipful flies, to a dusty country road. Then I'll head myself for Sarnath. It shouldn't be hard to find a hardy companion or two for some good ice block sitting. Maybe, I'll find some sari-clad maidens like my past women who just warmed me in their Indian guises. Heat and cold; black and white; dark and light; male and female; what I'm looking for is a balance. Hey, moderation was the path for Buddha.

CHOICES

"Bill, if we do not make another son, I must leave you."

Lei Carens sat straight and perfectly still in a high-backed cane chair, her small hands folded in her lap as she made this declaration, looking with an unwavering stare at her husband of ten years. Her jet-black hair was pulled back in a bun, giving her fine-boned face an imperious look. She was wearing an elegant sheath dress with a Mandarin collar. Bill had wondered out loud at dinner why she had dressed as if for a ceremonial occasion. She looked as lovely as she had on their wedding day.

Conversation during the meal had been sporadic. Soon after dinner Bill was slumped deep in the cushions of his favorite oversize couch by the picture window of their 25th-floor condo. The couch didn't match the dark reddish walls and lacquered antique furniture of the rest of the apartment but was a hard-won concession to his comfort.

He put a glass of Glenlivet on the coffee table in front of him. With his shirttail out and his worn slippers, he was as unkempt as Lei was elegant. His plan had been to enjoy the view of Victoria Harbour through the pleasant haze induced by the Glenlivet, then check some information on three antique bronzes from the Shane period he was considering adding to his beloved collection.

Then, Lei had set down in front of him and made her announcement. Bill shifted his heavy-set body on the couch, sitting up as tall as he could on the soft cushions. Although he had not prepared for this particular ultimatum, he was somehow not surprised. Their marriage had been going downhill since their little boy, Wenkai, died three years earlier after a lengthy illness. At first, they had worked hard together at absorbing and understanding the trauma of his death and the effect on their relationship, both by themselves and with the help of a therapist. These worthy efforts, instead of drawing them closer together, had the effect of fueling more rancorous discussion.

The most recent episode was typical. When she had come home the previous Saturday with an armful of shopping bags from one of Hong Kong's most fashionable stores, he, who had formerly loved to finance the task of enhancing her appearance, yelled, "You've got to stop this, Lei. You're killing us. I asked you to cut back. I told you I may lose my job."

"Well, I see you found the money for two more of those silly horses from the Tang Dynasty you couldn't live without," she countered in Mandarin. "You already have forty of them. Anyway these things are for Wenlai. She's eight now." Concluding in English, she said, "Getting bigger; needs new clothes."

"Ah, the guilt trip," he thrust back. And off they went for twenty minutes in Mandarin. After the anger had been temporarily spent, he looked at her sadly and said, "I wonder where all this is going. We can't seem to find a way of talking about anything without getting mad, can we?"

In a rare moment of accord, she nodded.

Now, as she sat across from him, he tried to stave off the inevitable, because he didn't know how to deal with it.

"Of course this is important, but I am not ready to talk right now. There's a lot else that needs to be taken into account here."

He paused and leaned back.

"I had another meeting with that young pain in the ass today, Reginald Jones. You've met Reginald. Quite fancied him I thought."

Lei didn't respond. He went on doing his rather inept best to imitate the English accent he found so condescending.

"Bill, you're fifty-five now. You've been a simply super member of the firm; appreciate your work so much. But, it might be nearing time for you to think about a future that doesn't rely so heavily on our great mistress, the law."

He sat back in disgust.

"I'd like to mistress that arrogant bastard. Those Brits have got something against American lawyers."

He threw up his hands in a gesture intended to settle the issue.

"How can we decide anything right now if I am going to lose my job? Look," he conceded, "I promise I'll think about it soon."

"Okay, I speak now. You never think good time to talk," she said in a quiet voice. "Always tired or something. But we must talk. And with thought too."

She smiled, he thought, to emphasize her willingness to be reasonable.

"We both have fault, and not nice to each other sometime. I know about job. But I think that work out. You are good lawyer."

She leaned toward him, emphasizing the next sentences.

"I am honest. I go crazy if we don't make decision now. My position not easy, but I believe it is only way I can stay with our marriage."

Bill had noted with surprise that she was speaking English. Her comprehension was fine, but her spoken English wasn't so good. Among other things she had an uneasy relation with various parts of speech and tended generally to leave them out, which made her sound quite stilted. She was most feisty and effective when they argued in her native tongue.

"Why are we talking in English? We've never talked much in English, let alone argue. Are you trying to get my sympathy or something?"

"No, I want to make my argument from my heart and not with easy language or getting angry. Anyway, this not argument. About position best for all of us, including both our children."

He was surprised at the reference to their dead son. How could a decision affect him?

"Okay." He ran his hand through thinning sandy hair and nodded a little skeptically. "Okay, I guess we have to talk about it. Look, I'll start. This part about you leaving me if we don't have a son. Aren't we going backward with that? We have a lovely daughter." He paused and went on. "And whatever you say, the timing is not so hot with this job thing."

He quickly finished his Glenlivet and went to get another one. Bill was over six foot two, weighed two hundred thirty pounds with an expanding paunch, and walked in a somewhat ungainly fashion, having a tendency to bump into the closely placed furniture.

Her gaze followed him as he moved across the room.

"Bill, please don't get drunk. We must discuss clearly. I want another son. You don't or you won't decide. You know I stop with birth control. What do you think happening?"

He poured the Glenlivet and walked back to the couch, carefully avoiding her chair.

"Well, I think we never talked about the birth control stuff, and you knew I was still using them." She didn't like him saying "condoms." "We never talked about that either. It wasn't like a mutual decision."

Then more aggressively he said, "Now all of a sudden you put everything in a whole different light."

"Sorry I not make it clearer. Sometime you a little stupid though. Don't see obvious things. Don't face up to things."

"I'm ready to face up when I know what I am supposed to be facing up to," he defended himself sharply. "Come on, you just haven't been clear about what you wanted, never mind the crazy reason why."

Bill pointed a finger at Lei.

"How about first things first? Don't you think we should decide if we have a basis for a decent marriage before we do anything else? Talk to a therapist? Search our hearts? Having another kid doesn't sound like a simple solution."

"Having another son," she gently corrected him. "We already see therapist. Search hearts top to bottom. Just end up fighting more."

"Lei, right after Wenkai died, I desperately wanted another child. You didn't. That was really hard, but I got used to the idea. We have our wonderful Wenlai. Why don't we leave the child part alone? It's in the past now."

He was angry and frustrated. Lei was walking down two diverging avenues at one time. A baby or a divorce. It didn't make sense. What about love and respect or at least some set of workable compromises.

He hauled himself off the couch and circled the room, bypassing the bar.

Lei didn't respond directly. Her glance went to her lap. She made a small cradle of her arms and, with a radiant look on her face, rocked the cradle back and forth.

"It never in past. Always with us. No one ever replace our little Wenkai. Precious boy always be with me, deep in me."

"Deep in you, too." She stopped rocking and looked at him. "I see having new son different now. Before too much pain to think about it. Only loss."

Bill noticed that while her face was sad, there was no sign of tears. She went on.

"A son needed to save our family. And save souls in the process. She looked up and included him. "Our souls; Wenkai's soul too."

Lei had never referred to anybody's soul in his presence before nor had he heard her make any reference to Chinese ways of dealing with death and honoring their ancestors if in fact that was what she was talking about. Wenkai wasn't an ancestor anyway. He scratched his head. Could a son who dies first be his own father's ancestor?

He found himself slumping again and straightened up. While she had been rocking the imaginary Wenkai, he had a clear and sweet memory of her rocking their real son as a tiny infant. He knew this was affecting him. It wasn't in the past. Who was he trying to kid?

He shook his head trying to keep sentiment away.

"We did have him baptized, you know."

She shrugged.

"That Western way. Maybe not enough for Chinese part of him or me."

He was amazed she was still speaking English and seemed so serene and sure of her ground.

"I don't know what you're talking about here; our souls; Wenkai's soul? What I do know is you're forty now and Dr. Wong said there could be serious risks for you and the baby if we did try to have another child. That was a while ago, too."

"We will have healthy boy."

Bill threw up his hands.

"What if it's a girl?"

"It will be boy."

"What about Dr. Wong?"

"Dr. Wong is old fart. I see Dr. Smithson now. He says I am healthy and strong. Average risk only. He will monitor everything carefully."

She spoke more softly now.

"This mean so much to Wenlai. She want little brother to love. You want son, too. You just forget. You wonderful father. I know job is worry, but you are smart man and will work out."

He felt she was casting some spell over him.

"Why hard to accept? Reasonable thing I suggest."

Bill was perplexed with this mystical approach from one who always favored hard-edged debate. He continued to question.

"You make it all sound easy. Anyway," he said, cupping his hand around his ear, "I don't hear suggestion. I hear ultimatum."

"Bill, I have much agony over this which I do not share."

She reached out toward him.

"I think this hard to understand, but I believe some voice telling me without a new son to replace Wenkai, we are not family anymore, and without family there is not marriage for me."

Bill put his head in his hands.

"You loved Wenkai. The two of us make another son. Not just for me. For all of us."

Bill pushed himself to his feet and began pacing back and forth in front of the room-length window looking out on Victoria Harbour. He had stopped drinking. His hair was tousled and his face flushed. Lei continued to sit calmly in the cane-backed chair, which had to be uncomfortable. He hated the feeling he was being manipulated and made one more attempt to win the day.

"If you're ready to divorce, why don't you just get a divorce and find another man to have a child with? Why do you want me to be the father? Yeah, look at me. I'm fifty-five years old, getting too fat, and about to be fired."

He pinched the layer of fat around his belly.

"Maybe not so good in bed anymore either. I'm not a goddamn stud you know."

"You are just not understanding me. Not about sex. Actually I like to make love with you. Good even if angry sometimes. What I do with another man not even a thought. I can only have the family I want with you."

She stood up for the first time since the conversation started and looked at him without blinking or turning away.

"I would be making big sacrifice if I leave you and give up last chance for a son made of our blood. It is duty—duty to ourselves, to daughter, and to Wenkai. Our duty to remain family. I know I don't talk this way much but you must trust me."

Bill couldn't stop himself. Stuff that hasn't surfaced for a long time came out.

"Okay, okay. Big as this family thing is, don't you and I need something more for ourselves? We all hear voices. My voice says to me we fight a lot; that you married out of love but also because I was a passport out of Beijing to a pretty good lifestyle."

For the first time Lei showed anger and cursed in Mandarin, then caught herself and continued in English.

"I married you because I love you. Yes, I proud you successful lawyer and generous man. Why not? I was poor." She paused. "But this a lot more than shopping and nice flat. Marriage not easy. Marriage not perfect. I want to stay married and try to be happy. Child very important but you very important person for me too."

Lei began to cry. This was unheard of. She took out a handkerchief and dabbed at her eyes.

"We have to decide now. Please, Bill, say yes to a new son. Why you not say yes?"

"Okay, that's enough. I need to think."

He put his hand on her shoulder for a second and said, "I'm going upstairs."

As he headed up to bedroom floor, he said, "Why don't I sleep in the guest room so I can think better and you can sleep better? Okay?"

Lei hesitated and then nodded yes.

Bill was powerfully tempted to lie down and rest a little. Maybe he was just too old and jaded for all this. But he knew that he had to think some more. He chose a hard, straight-backed chair and set it by the window so he could see the harbor. Even at eleven o'clock there were still many boats scurrying back and forth; many missions still to be accomplished. He was distracted and, at the same time, refreshed by the unceasing pulsing of life in Hong Kong.

Tonight his prickly, unpredictable, beautiful wife had found a new mode of expression: English, souls, softness, ancestors, duty to family. A transformation so radical and new that he wondered if he could really trust what she said. He wondered if she was really as convinced of what she proposed as she sounded.

Beneath her mysterious manner, Bill decided there was a genuine core. If what she wanted was a divorce, she could just ask for it without all the other business. If she would only stay with him if they had another son, despite her stress on the family part, there had to be some love for him. She had as much as said so.

For that matter what did he really think of her? Breaking up had crossed his mind on numerous occasions when they couldn't stop fighting. He was pretty sure that love was still there for him, blunted though it might be by the hard times they had had. Given the way their lives were going, he couldn't expect much more from himself and her.

He thought back to the days right after Wenkai died and how much he wanted his son back in his life. The desire had abated. He had lost will and let self-pity wash over him, knocking him this way and that. Sometimes he thought all he really cared about was his collection of bronzes: uncomplicated objects he could simply admire.

Tonight for the first time in ages, he could feel some life beating inside, buried beneath the layers built up by just going along. Whatever it was, the need for a son like Lei or some other need of his, long repressed, something was stirring. There was still a lot of thinking to be done.

Bill had heard Lei go to their bedroom, pausing at his door and then moving on. He continued to look down at the harbor. The boats still hurried about. It was difficult to discern a pattern to what they were doing. As difficult, he supposed, as detecting a pattern in his own life.

He tiptoed into the bedroom, undressed, put on his pajamas and climbed into bed. Lei was already sound asleep. Bill guessed she was clear in her mind about what she had proposed. He didn't want to wake her.

FRED AND ME

My name is Norman Greenfield. I first became acquainted with Fred at Mercy Hospital near Binghamton, New York, where I was undergoing treatment for schizophrenia, yet again. Back in because my meds weren't quite right and neighbors who had been short in stature and friendly grew in size and started staring at me suspiciously. But this stay was different, as you will see. This time I met Fred.

Superintendent Charles Burlingame, a conscientious and capable professional, had been in charge of Mercy for fifteen years. He has recently expanded the hospital's range by starting the Mercy Hospital Parrot Institute (the "PI"), satisfying some sort of mid-career, mid-life need, I suppose. Fred was one of several African Gray Parrots in the first class at PI being trained to serve the mentally ill.

I was selected by Superintendent Burlingame to have responsibility for Fred's care and feeding during off-duty hours. Burlingame knew me well because this was my third visit during his tenure. He respected my intelligence when it was not thrown off-kilter by schizophrenia. We had discovered during my first visit that we were both avid readers of very serious fiction. On occasion, we would read the same novel (one recent example was Anna Karenina) and exchange views. We often met in his office; that gave me the welcome feeling of being special.

Fred was medium-sized with a gray body, dark-gray wings, and a light-gray rump. This varied grayness contrasted nicely with his black beak and cherry-red tail. He was the most intelligent in his class, the dominant personality, and by far the handsomest. He was so full of energy and song and joy, and he flew when freed of his cage with such fire and soaring spirit that my heart wanted to levitate with him. And he had a clear, strong ego that I, with my dark complexities, wished I could emulate. We seemed to hit it off right away, were on a "Fred" and "Norman" basis almost from the start.

Fred and the other parrots in training had their homes in cages in the recreation hall commonly called the "Wreck." The room was appropriately askew, containing some broken-down couches, several listing lamps, assorted mismatched chairs, and heavily varnished paintings of prior superintendents of Mercy, most of these tipped at one angle or another and quite dusty. The parrots' cages were in the south corner amid a small forest of artificial palms, their rubber leaves stained yellow by the sun. The trees reminded me of the lobby of the cheap Broadway hotel that I frequented during one of my lapses back into society. The caramel-colored walls—undraped, streaked windows—and scuffed brown carpet completed the picture of institutional flatness. It was in this setting that the first really close relationship I had with any creature improbably flourished.

As to the rationale for the PI, African Grays have been found to be helpful companions, not just to the blind but to persons with mental illness trying to make it on their own. The best of the Grays have proven capable of quite incredible feats of language and abstract thinking, particularly when you consider that their brains are no bigger than a walnut. You may know of the parrot named Alex, trained by Dr. Irene Pepperberg, and his ability to speak, count, pick out colors, and even (although there is not unanimity on this point) understand the concept of "zero." Alex died suddenly before he had a chance to realize his full potential. Early in our relationship I felt that Fred, given world enough and time, would exceed Alex's achievements.

Much of Fred's day was spent in academia, in a specially equipped room in the basement where he and the other qualified parrots were being trained in the latest techniques for assisting mental patients. Training was done by a tall, blond man called Pete, fiercely dedicated to his work and seemingly more fond of parrot than human company.

…ut seven each morning and lift off the
…light and dampened his song to an oc-
…ng the long, dark night. The hood seemed
…without it sleep was difficult. As the hood as-
…ne day with great bursts of noise. I tried to cho-
…iting periodically, "Good morning, Fred. Every-
…ort time, he could respond with a decent facsimile
…Norman. Okay, okay." I would open the cage door
…flash, taking his laps around the room (a necessity for a
…ly) while I prepared his breakfast of nuts and fruit. I loved
…in which he attacked his meals after his workout. His man-
ners, …ch I could never change, were abominable, but his pleasure, as he
tore, scratched, bullied, and consumed his food, was palpable. After dining,
while we waited for classes to start, he would happily chew new bits off a
multi-limbed wooden toy in his cage.

In class Pete taught the parrots such things as how to remind patients
it was time to take medication, how to make a ssshhhing noise imitating
the sound of running water if their charge forgot to turn off the water faucet or neglected to flush the toilet, how to guide a shaky one through the
confusion and stress of city traffic with a series of vocal signals and a variety
of other useful skills, including phrases to calm down a disturbed person
like, well, "Calm down!" or "Relax." I would help him do his homework,
practicing some of his phrasing and reminders on me. I didn't need reminders about toilet flushing. But, faithfully, I would stand in the dark toilet
with Fred at my side while he would go, "Ssshhhh! Ssshhhh! Ssshhhh!"
with such vigor and persistence that I finally had to say, "Fred, I flushed
already! If you don't stop that, I'll 'ssshhhh' you."

In the evening, after Fred consumed more nuts and fruit and sharpened
his claws on his favorite abrasive pad, I would reluctantly lower the black hood
over his cage, postponing the moment as long as I could, and he would commence the slow process of going to sleep, not without petulant cries, like a child
whose bedtime story was not long enough. Our day was over.

We could talk together about things. We really could. One afternoon stands out. I was sitting outside his cage, Fred perched quietly on my hand, unusually pensive.

I said, "Fred, where did you come from anyway?" I thought of his parents perched on some moss-covered ruin in the moist heat of a Congo jungle. Fred's responding vocalization was something I hadn't heard before. I thought I detected a whiff of sadness, of melancholy in his tone.

To cheer him up, I said, "Do you know that people had parrots as companions four thousand years ago. Huh? Isn't that something! The Egyptians, the Greeks, the Romans! They all loved parrots. The Romans had these really beautiful ornate cages." I thought to myself I wouldn't promise him but someday I'd like to get him a fancy, fancy cage. "Listen to this, Fred: If you lived four hundred years ago, you might have been Henry the Eighth's favorite parrot! Or, a little bit earlier than that you could have sailed with Vasco da Gama around the Cape of Good Hope."

I thought he looked happier, hearing about his proud lineage, but then wondered if he felt he was missing out.

"Fred, I hope you're not unhappy here at Mercy, here with me," I dared venture.

Then, all of a sudden I started telling him about myself. He listened patiently while I told him my life history: my childhood on a farm near Binghamton surrounded by books; a compromised mother and a stern, unloving father; the skinny student with big glasses; the loner who read, read, and read more the older and more lonely he got; the sudden onset of schizophrenia in my senior year of college just before graduation from Columbia as an English major; and the long struggles thereafter, fighting my illness and trying to live a half-normal life. Maybe not a unique story but it was my real story.

During my revelations, I felt from Fred what I can only call empathy. He showed no signs of impatience during these serious moments so I kept on going, talking about my mother's drinking and stumbling around the kitchen, dropping food all over the floor. I started to cry a little. Finally realizing I was talking about something he really couldn't possibly understand, I brushed away the tears and smiled at him. But Fred did look as if he understood and seemed sympathetic. I was very touched. I found it so easy to talk freely with him.

My own condition improved in direct proportion to the time I spent with Fred. Jane Petersen, who was my therapist, commented favorably on how well I was doing and what loving care I took of Fred. "This is doing you a lot of good. You're getting very stable," she said with pleasure at one of our sessions. I nodded. But I couldn't tell her that my experience with Fred was going beyond stabilization and into an area I had never been before with another living creature.

I was so swept up with his fearlessness, his joy in living. The best time we had, short-lived thought it was, was our pirate game. Growing up as I did, constricted and far from the bounding main, my fantasies roamed the seven seas with carefree pirates in search of treasure. I read Treasure Island as a boy several times. As I became interested in Fred, Superintendent Burlingame encouraged me to read it again. I had at some point in my young adult life actually purchased an appropriate costume. It was a very authentic-appearing outfit complete with eye patch, feathered tri-cornered hat, a wooden peg leg, a wooden cutlass painted silver and other accoutrements. But, I was without the key ingredient: a parrot.

Somehow this outfit had been packed in a compartment of my suitcase long ago and traveled with me undisturbed and forgotten. Meeting Fred rekindled the old passion, and I had, from time to time in the privacy of my room, dressed in the outfit and swashbuckled around a bit. At first I thought it wouldn't be appropriate as Fred's mentor to involve him, tempting as it was. But, he watched me avidly and, after a bit, I felt it was silly to resist.

Once I broke through the wall of my reserve, new and wonderful things happened. I christened myself Calico Jack Greenfield; dressed in my splendid uniform, my faithful parrot on my shoulder and sang out to him to join me in feeling the surge of the waves under the deck and inhaling the scent of booty on the brisk, salty wind. Then Fred, whose pirate name remained Fred, and I, armed with my cutlass, would sashay back and forth around my room. I cried, "Avast there! Your money or your life," while skewering the helpless cot and single metal chair in the room. Fred, quick as always (piracy is no doubt in the Gray's genome), embraced our game and contributed mightily, after a little vocal priming, with, "Pieces of eight, Pieces of eight," or, "Fie, you swabbies." When I looked in the mirror after our plundering raids, I saw the robust, wind-reddened visage of a seafarer, not the gaunt body and thin face with deep, haunted eyes of the thirty-eight-year-old social misfit that usually greeted me.

I was fully aware that this activity would not be countenanced outside my room. However, Fred was forever at the door, yearning to be free. Finally, one day I got caught up in his enthusiasm and together our spirits flew out of the room's confines in joyous violation, our bodies following close behind. Calico Jack Greenfield and his companion sallied forth into the hallways and even as far as the Wreck, threatening inmates, slashing without mercy at the ragged couches and listing lamps. This palpable breaking of the rules was one of the high moments of my life. But all too quickly our days on the high seas were over. The guards arrived and we were led back to port.

Soon I was summoned to Superintendent Burlingame's office.

"Norman, I have to say I am very disappointed. Robert Louis Stevenson and all of that. I'm afraid I had something to do with this." He shook his head. "Anyway you certainly know better than to do rush about with a sword, screaming at the top of your lungs. Dammit! You scared some of the patients out of their wits!" He paused on that for a moment and looked at me as severely as he could. "I'm surprised at you. No more of that, right."

"That was certainly thoughtless. I'm sorry. We just got carried away," I said.

"It's not the kind of training I want Fred to have," he went on. "He's our best. He's going to make us all very proud of the Mercy Hospital Parrot Institute."

I had the strange feeling Superintendent Burlingame was trying to repress a smile and the thought his heart isn't really in this reprimand.

"Well, I wasn't going to get in the situation with you and Fred but here we are," he resumed. "This, ah, unusual action of yours doesn't change my mind. We'll put it behind us. Okay?"

I nodded. Of course that was okay with me, whatever he was about to say.

"A lot of the reason Fred is doing so well is you, Norman. I've noticed how helpful taking responsibility for Fred has been for you. And how Fred has blossomed and so have you. You're a great pair." He leaned back, smiling broadly. "I've been thinking about this for a while. Jane and Pete agree with me." He leaned over toward me and lowered his voice, appearing to feel some need to preserve the confidentiality of what he was about to say.

"Norman, you're not the type of person I expected to send out with my first Gray. You're probably more able to take care of yourself than most despite your comings and goings here. And certainly among the most intelligent." He coughed again. "At least when you are yourself and not running around in a pirate costume. Anyway, you could make it alone, I'm convinced, this time. But you two seem so close that I want you to have Fred with you when you leave. You're the ideal pair to show the world what we are doing here at PI."

My heart started beating faster. Frankly I hadn't thought much about not being with Fred or hadn't wanted to but the possibility was frightening as it now sprang to mind so I barely heard him say, almost to himself, "It'll be a great start for the program" but did hear him go on with "In fact, come to think of it, given the problem with your meds the last time out, it seems exactly the thing to do." He looked at me hard. "What do you think?"

I wanted to give this kindly man a hug but just nodded.

He came around from behind the desk, and as I got up he put his hand on my shoulder. "I think both of you are doing well enough that in a couple of months or so, you ought to be able to leave together." As I reached the door, he raised a warning hand and said, "Remember! No more Long John Silver."

"I was actually Calico Jack Greenfield."

"Okay, whatever. Good luck, Norman."

Thrilled, I ran to communicate the information to Fred. He seemed to share my delight and began screaming, "Pieces of eight! Pieces of eight!" at full volume. I took him to my room to quiet down.

We did continue to play in the room but Fred had liked our one foray so much he would go to the door and then return to seize my shirt with his beak, trying to drag me to the outside. "Pieces of eight! Pieces of eight!" he would cry plaintively. And I would have to disappoint him. Frankly, too, for some reason I had lost interest in the game. Heady as our brief fling was, we were about to enter a more realistic world together and I had to be ready. The pirate experience became a salutary lesson in boundaries and limitations for me.

Over the ensuing weeks, my mood remained elevated and steady. Having someone I wanted to be with was a new and wonderful experience. I started using endearments like "baby." Soon I went further, whispering, "Love you," to him in the morning upon waking and at night before our final, "Night, night." He would look at me and repeat it. I do have to say though that I often caught myself thinking that it wasn't quite right to feel this way about a parrot. But, then I said to myself, "The hell with it. This is the nicest time you've ever had."

A few days before my release, I had another meeting with Superintendent Burlingame, this time with Fred in attendance.

"This will be a major, major transition for you, Norman. You'll be on your own. Well, of course," he smiled paternally, gazing at Fred who remained passive but I knew was pleased, "you'll have the pride of the PI as your assistant. You've gone out before but we really want it to work this time. I want you to be prepared."

I nodded.

"You know Frank Abrams, the head of 'Outside Programs'?"

Of course I did.

Not waiting for an answer, he continued, "Frank and his people will look in on you periodically, but we need you to take as much responsibility as possible." I noticed that Fred was listening to Superintendent Burlingame very intently.

"I want you to think about what you're going to do when you're out on your own completely. You're a bright man and you've got your degree in English Lit, right?"

He glanced at me and I confirmed his statement with a nod.

"But I'm afraid, for now…hmm…with your background, a teaching job is out." He paused and sighed, "One of these days, I hope society will recognize how valuable people like you can be. I can see you in a library though. Love of books and all. Quiet and not stressful." He paused. Then, he leaned forward to spring his surprise, smiling with pleasure. "And that's where you'll be working two afternoons a week, in the local library near Benedict House. Starting in your second month." He sat back, visibly delighted with his news.

I was about to ask about Fred when he raised his hand to stop me and said, "We have permission for you to bring Fred with you, at least some of the time. Of course, he will have to be pretty quiet. That'll be your responsibility"

"Thanks so much, sir!" I finally said.

A week later, the doors of Mercy opened, and, with Fred beside me in a slick, new stainless steel cage (a gift from Jane), we set out on our new adventure together. It was a superb June day. Jane, Superintendent Burlingame, Pete, and a number of staff members and even patients were there to send us off. The superintendent made a brief speech, congratulating Fred for being the first graduate of PI, lauding Pete for his excellent work, and wishing us, man and parrot, bon voyage. Then, he handed me Fred's diploma to the applause of the onlookers.

Jane looked hopeful and a little tearful. Pete looked sad. He had said to me the night before when I went to the basement to help pack Fred's things, "You have a natural gift for this. Much more than most of the other helpers." And he told me, "Burlingame is very happy about the way this is going. This is the biggest thing he has done in fifteen years here. And he's got his eye on you."

Even at this happy time, this remark made me a little shaky. There had been talk of my responsibilities that chafed even as it warmed my opinion of myself. But I knew Pete's remark was meant as a compliment.

As I was about to leave, Pete put his hand on my shoulder, looked at me hard and said, "Be good to this guy, Norman. He's my first graduate and the best in his class." It occurred to me that Pete was jealous, maybe even in love with Fred, too. I wondered what Pete had given Fred for last minute instructions.

"Here's home, baby." I lifted Fred's cage in my arms and stepped over the threshold. Fred responded to this romantic moment by squawking, "Meds! Meds! Meds!" I had hoped for something a little more intimate.

"Come on, Fred," I said, "you can do better than that, silly. I already took them. You watched me." I rattled the cage a little. "Come on! Let's look at our new home."

He persisted with his instructions and I said as quietly as I could, "Calm down!" He started to repeat this, looked a little perturbed, and stopped.

I opened the door of the cage. "Okay, fly around and pick out where you want the cage to be."

Whether he understood the exact message or not, he circled the living room twice and then settled down on a plain wood table next to the back window. "Okay," I said, "we'll set you right over this." I put the new cage on the table. "I'll hang it later. Nice place, eh, Fred?"

Our apartment was on a quiet side street in Binghamton, small and minimally but adequately furnished. The building was a halfway house owned by Mercy called the Benedict House. I had a six- month transitional time here, a period that surprised me with its generous length.

After my gray, sparse quarters at Mercy, our apartment was lovely, light, and pleasant. The rooms had been freshly wallpapered. The windows were clean. Both of our rooms had views out the back window of a pretty garden with a couple of lounge chairs under a tall sugar maple. I was filled with optimism and the desire to make a comfortable life for the two of us.

With my small allowance I purchased a woven rug with alternating streaks of dark and light gray and spots of black and cherry red, Fred's colors, for the living room. Also, I purchased a pair of lamps with small birds, unfortunately not parrots, perched on the base. I hung Fred's diploma on the wall near his cage where both of us could see it. I parrot-proofed the bedroom and living room so he had good air space for flying since he could not fly unfettered outside. I had no intention of clipping his wings to limit flight capacity. Pete thought, and I agreed, this was an abominable practice, taking away the bird's freedom.

Fred spent most of the day out of the cage, even when I was not there. When not investigating or playing with his toys, he would perch near me, content to watch while I read and did my stress management exercises, important for a schizophrenic if he wants to keep straight. We carried on our funny stilted sort of conversation, sort of like old married people, throughout the day. I did read a great deal, having decided to read Dostoevsky. I had wanted to read him in the past but had been a little afraid because of what I understood to be the powerfully complex and often destructive personalities that abounded in his writing and what they might do to my psychological state. However I was so emboldened by the changes in my life, I was determined to do it.

Fred wanted to play the pirate game, but I really had lost interest. It seemed a little childish and brought back memories of being called to Superintendent Burlingame's office. Plus, now that I had my own place I didn't want to risk damaging the furniture. Fred took this hard, I must say, but seemed to get over it. In that same vein about keeping a neat and tidy home, sometimes I needed to rein in his exuberant behavior, much as I hated to. For instance, one day we had a strained time when he began to chew on the couch cushions and I had to caution him. "This is your apartment too, Fred! Come on." I did try not to be too fussy and remembered that Fred was a parrot.

We walked every day. Fred had to stay in his cage, a frustration, but necessary for his safety. Food and other supplies were available at a nearby shop run by an elderly gentleman, Mr. Jamison, who was particularly helpful and nice. Benedict House occupants were still somewhat of a novelty in the neighborhood and the neighborhood was certainly a novelty for Fred. A few folks lamely tried, "Polly, Polly! Look, little Jimmy, look. Say, 'Polly want a cracker?'" Fred had not heard these clichés before, and fortunately they didn't happen often enough for him to add them to his vocabulary.

I found myself talking with some of the other residents and developed cordial relations with a couple of men about my age. This was a happy surprise, and I took it to be one of the many benefits of my relationship with Fred. Just by being himself he had done so much to bring me out of the thick antisocial shell that had accreted over my thirty-five years. But, mainly, I was quite content to be with Fred, and he seemed to be the same with me, although sometimes I felt he may have missed the companionship and his high stature at the PI. He was sometimes saucy, sometimes affectionate, generally a good listener, often vocal and noisy, particularly when he was hungry. Never dull. Our occasional disagreements over meal times and cleanliness seemed, at first, a natural consequence of two beings living in close proximity. I felt I had found something as close to happiness as I ever would.

After a month, I began my volunteer work at the library. Part of my time was spent in the children's section, and naturally the children loved Fred. He would preen and jump around his cage while they squealed with delight, to such an extent that I teased him about being a "big showoff." Knowing I was supposed to keep him under control, I worried that he was too exuberant, but no one seemed to be concerned.

My work was picking books up and filing them—not much of a challenge but pleasant enough. The staff was very nice and helpful, particularly a woman about my age named Margaret Sutton, a single woman.

Margaret didn't look like a librarian. No glasses or hair pulled back in a bun. Sometimes she wore un-sensible shoes, let her brown hair fall down to her shoulders, and dressed as if she were going to a party right after work. I was shy around her at first but soon, helped by my newfound social skills, could talk with her quite easily. Margaret seemed to enjoy my company and our conversation. Again I thought to myself that I had never been able to do that before and that I had Fred with his sense of fun and joy in life to thank for this happy change in my life.

Frank Abrams stopped by every other week and announced he was pleased with how our life was going. The summer days passed quickly and, at the end of two months, it was time for us to check in at the hospital. I took Fred to Pete's office and left him for a visit, went for some tests, and then met with Jane. We concluded our visit by meeting with Superintendent Burlingame. He was quite pleased with how things were going. He asked in particular how Fred and I were getting along and looked satisfied but became a little nonplussed when I waxed, perhaps a little too enthusiastically, about our life as a couple—how much fun we had together, how happy we were. "We, we, we…" and on and on I went.

"Norman, this all sounds fine," he finally interrupted. "And I know how good you and Fred are together. Let's not forget though that Fred is a service animal," he cautioned. "His job is basically to help you stay on track. Companionship is fine. We just want to be sure he's doing his job, what he's trained to do." He cleared his throat. "Lots of taxpayer dollars went into his, uh, training."

"Fred is doing his job and then some," I hastily reassured him. He looked relieved. I felt guilty later that I hadn't told him the full truth. That I wasn't really relying at all on Fred for guidance in my routine. I didn't need him for that. Our relationship was on a much higher plane.

The next two months continued at much the same pleasant level as summer ended and fall arrived, with its shorter days and crisper weather. On our walks I'd kick at the maple and oak leaves cluttering the sidewalks, scattering their reds and golds in showers before us, and Fred would squawk delightedly. When we got back to the apartment, me with rosy cheeks and Fred exhilarated, we'd dance around the living room. At these moments our relationship was a continuing miracle to me.

Our second visit to Mercy passed uneventfully. Frank Abrams, after his visits, always said he was pleased with how it was going. Then, November arrived with its ever earlier darkness. We had our fun and many happy moments. But more and more often I felt I wanted more time to sit in my chair by the window and read. We'd play for what seemed to me to be forever and after we'd finished, Fred would pester me to keep going.

"Fred, please leave me alone. Let me read. Come on, we just spent a whole lot of time playing." I guess he was like a little child who can never get enough of a game. I used to love this freshness and unvarying enthusiasm, but it was wearing a little thin now sometimes.

More and more, too, now that the relative silence of years had been broken, I found myself wanting to talk and talk beyond what was really a kind of baby talk. One day when I wasn't at the library I really wanted to talk about Brothers Karamazov. In frustration, I actually said to Fred, "Why do you think young Alyosha is such a damn saint?" and felt annoyance when he just gave me a silly look. I wanted to discuss the brothers and anger and the terrible things that went on between them and Father Karamazov.

I was still able to talk with Margaret in a way and with a depth that amazed me. Our chairs behind the counter were fairly close together (I was now signing books in and out). I liked the way she would lean over to make a remark to me and her fresh, soft smell. When I asked her about the Brothers Karamazov and how wild they all seemed she said with the most sympathetic look on her face, "What a sad situation that was. All that…." She paused and then said, "Turmoil and strife, those self-inflicted wounds." I was sure for a moment she was on the verge of saying "craziness" and had refrained out of decency. She knew about my situation of course, and I knew she knew, but we didn't discuss it.

I said, "Yeah, they were pretty much all manic. You could say crazy." I just felt like saying it. I looked at her. She blushed and turned away to stack some books.

I thought a lot about responsibility. I felt responsible for Fred and certainly to Superintendent Burlingame and Jane who had supported me so strongly. But I couldn't stop thinking about all the expectation about Fred and me and my successful reentry into society; the two of us carrying the banner of the PI out into the world. The fact that Fred wasn't really helping me like he had been trained to do was going to come out one of these days. As the days grew shorter, these thoughts morphed into high, black walls with no handholds. Sometimes I looked at Fred and felt resentful of his freedom. He had no idea what went on in my head, no idea what a human being had to live with.

As for Fred, I don't think he noticed any difference in me. He did seem on occasion to be less eager for my company. At the library, he remained in prime form, a born ham, and I still enjoyed the way the children responded to him. But I chided him one evening for being livelier with them than he was with me. I began to think he was a distraction; keeping the children from their reading; getting them all agitated. I exercised the discretion that Superintendent Burlingame had requested and started leaving Fred at the apartment one afternoon a week. Another reason, frankly, was that he'd kick up a big fuss looking for attention if I was talking to Margaret. The library staff accepted my explanation about Fred being a distraction. I had the feeling that they had become disenchanted with him themselves.

Fred took this hard, and I could feel his mood darkening. He stopped flying around with his former abandon and his always hearty appetite diminished. He stopped sharpening his claws on his pad and toys and let them grow long. Now when I approached, scissors in hand, for a trimming, he would strike a threatening posture that I knew meant he was ready to bite to defend his bodily integrity.

Even at this point when I was angry with Fred I thought of what he had given me, what he had taught me about life and having a sense of joy.

Then I felt guilty, blamed myself and tried to apologize to him, then confused everything by asking myself what I was doing. He was just a parrot, and oh, my god, I didn't mean that, and on it went. Then I'd blame him for my deteriorating condition and the ill will that was becoming palpable between us. I started having dark thoughts about Superintendent Burlingame, who had really been so good to me, and cursed him for starting PI and using me as his prize guinea pig. The cycle of black thinking just went round and round with no conclusion.

Two more weeks passed and things got worse. I could hardly go to the store anymore because the fragile Mr. Jamison was beginning to assume a lethal and threatening size. At home I could see fresh yellowish stains erupting daily on the wallpaper that I couldn't seem to wipe off. The waning daylight, harsh and stark, coming through the windows made the everyday furniture of the room into menacing objects.

Frank Abrams began appearing less often and seemed pretty indifferent when he did. I kept going to the library with Fred one day a week because I knew not to do so would arouse suspicion. Then I called and said I had the flu and wouldn't be in for a while. Around the apartment more I became more morose and suspicious, Fred's service instincts, rusty through disuse, for some strange reason, began to reemerge. He made one last effort to be professional.

"Cheer up! Calm down! Relax! Meds! Meds!"

He tried his whole range of options, but his very persistence began to give me a headache. In particular, the "meds" part annoyed me because I knew I was taking them. Maybe something was wrong but that wasn't the problem.

At night behind the safety of a closed door I would lie in bed and reflect on the good times we had had and whether there was any way they could be salvaged. Frequently I cried. But in the morning, the hostilities would commence as I fearfully jerked the hood off his cage and saw him glaring angrily at me if I was late, which was often.

One morning he started greeting me by crying, "Pete, Pete," and "Where's Pete?" which hurt my feelings.

"Hey, I'm the one taking care of you!" I responded.

Finally, one late November afternoon, matters came to a head. After a day of his hectoring coupled with what I felt were honest attempts on my part to improve relations, I couldn't stand it any longer and left the house, leaving Fred in his cage. I had made one last try at pleasing him: I served him his favorite lunch, but he ate very little and threw the rest all over the cage.

"Don't like! Don't like," he screeched and screamed at me.

I said nothing until I got to the door. Then I turned and shouted back at him, "Walnut brain!"

I went through the streets, dazed, in a cold sweat. It had been a pleasant afternoon but now rain clouds were massing overhead. When I got home, he began immediately rattling his cage with renewed ferocity and glaring so fiercely I was afraid to let him out. I had a sudden urge to put on my pirate outfit, a hope that it might fortify my spirits. I took a look in the mirror after I had dressed and resembled more a prisoner about to walk the plank than the jaunty Calico Jack Greenfield. I staggered into the living room and slumped in an armchair. Fred gave out a series of squawks that made me think he was laughing at me, telling me I looked ridiculous.

He continued an essentially unintelligible harangue but then began to squawk something more recognizable. At first I thought he might be saying, "Let's do pirate!" I shook my head fiercely. As I listened I realized he was back on his "med" theme again.

"Meds! Meds! Meds!" Hesitatingly at first, then more and more rapidly in an increasingly raucous voice, he was badgering me now like he had never done before. My grip on sanity was sliding. I summoned all the courage I could to hold myself together, to suppress the rage and fear filling me up, ready to spill out all over the room.

"Fred, you know I'm taking the meds. Admit it." My voice sounded as if it was coming from outside my body. "Do you think that's helpful advice right now? Why don't you do something to help me?"

He wouldn't stop. Just kept hammering away, a sound growing louder and louder, like a great whirring drill descending ever closer to the top of my head, about to split it open. "Meds! Meds! Meds! Meds! Meds! Meds! Meds!" A saint could not have stood it.

I went in the bedroom and held my hands over my ears. No relief. The drumming in my head was pounding my slim remaining store of reason to bits. The son of a bitch was remarkable, but I wasn't going to take this from a goddamn parrot.

I returned to the living room. Fred looked at me hard and accusingly and tore away viciously at what was left of some cardboard fiber he had been systematically demolishing. I knew he wished it was me. There was quiet but the storm was at full strength. The moment had come.

I picked up the wooden cutlass. He began his taunting refrain again. I opened the cage which he was rattling harder and harder and stepped back, holding the weapon in a threatening position. Fred took off well out of reach, flying in broad circles.

"Hey, walnut brain! Come on," I taunted. He was flying in ever tighter circles and with each circle he seemed to be gaining in size and ferocity until I felt I was about to do battle with a mighty eagle on some high mountain peak. I knew an attack was imminent, whirled the cutlass over my head, and kept wheeling about to keep him in view. He tried to penetrate my defense. Finally, my arm growing weary, I moved toward the front door, opened it, and went on the offensive, trying to drive Fred outside without much success until on one of my wheels and swings the flat of the blade caught him hard. He fell to the floor, silenced and stunned.

What had I done? I was immediately torn between an urge to let him lie and wanting to rush to his side. While I was caught in this indeterminate state, Fred solved the problem. He shook his ruffled feathers and summoned the strength to flop weakly out the door. It was raining hard outside.

I was too wrought up to follow. I threw the offending cutlass aside, walked across the room, and collapsed in the armchair where I sat motionless and lost track of time. Darkness fell. Suddenly there was a loud knock on the door. Before I could get up, the door slammed open and Frank Abrams came in, striding purposefully, followed by two members of his team.

"Come on, Norman. You're heading back to the hospital." He noticed my disheveled costume. "And what the hell are you wearing there?" His two associates each took an arm to make sure I wouldn't do anything violent and lifted me out of the chair.

I yelled to Frank, who had gone into the bedroom to get my belongings. "He was after me."

When he came out, he was holding a full bottle of pills. "Hey, Norman, what happened, you missed these?"

I looked in horror and responded without thinking. "It's Fred's fault!"

Frank said, "Come on, Norman!" Then he whispered something to one of his assistants, like, "Burlingame going to be bullshit about this!"

The assistant responded, "Wait until Pete finds out!"

"What happened to Fred?" Frank asked. "One of your neighbors found him sitting all wet in his yard. He couldn't seem to fly. The guy recognized him from your walks and called Mercy to find out what he should do." We stood at the door, ready to go out. "We just picked him up. He's pretty beat up but I think he'll be okay."

"Thank God," I sobbed. The whole excruciating event was catching up with me. I don't remember the ride back to Mercy.

When I was wheeled into the hospital, I dimly remember noting that Superintendent Burlingame, who had always greeted me upon arrival in the past was not around. Jane was there, though. I remember little of the next few days except a blur of doctors and nurses and being wheeled up and down endless corridors. It was a bad, bad time. One night I was sure I heard a couple of nurses saying that the State was coming to investigate the incident and what was going at the PI. Later I had a vision of Superintendent

Burlingame outside the door, maybe with a knife in his hand. And another time I thought Pete was in my room circling the bed, clenching and un-clenching his fists, ready to attack me.

After about a week I was propped up in bed on some pillows, my mind clearing and beginning to return to a reality full of painful memories. Jane came in and said, "Well, Norman, I think we have figured out what happened." I nodded for her to continue.

"It turns out that you were taking most of the meds that you were supposed to but were missing out on one of them for maybe a month. Plus," she went on, "I want to talk to you some when you feel better about your stress levels and how things were between you and Fred."

She stopped to get my reaction. I shivered involuntarily and managed a weak, "I did the best I could."

"I'm sure you did. Sometimes we just can't predict how a situation will work out. I'm sure you're disappointed but we'll work on this together."

"What about Fred? Can I see him? Apologize or something. I don't know what I want to do?" I waved my hands around inconclusively. "I think I just want to cry."

"Norman, the best thing right now is for you to concentrate on getting yourself back in shape." She hesitated and leaned over closer. "Fred is getting great care and he'll be fine."

"Is he here? Why can't I see him?" I sat straight up in my bed. "What's he saying?"

"Norman, calm down please," she said sternly. "He's not here. He's going to be fine!"

I didn't believe her.

Jane got up to leave. I knew she was anxious to go.

"I'm glad you're feeling better. We'll start regular meetings again in a few day."

"What about Superintendent Burlingame? Why hasn't he come by?"

Jane just shook her head. I was back into reality enough to know that answer without asking. I sagged back on my pillows.

Jane smiled as encouragingly as she could and was half way out the door when I asked, "Has Margaret called from the library?"

She nodded her head, her face expressionless, and then left, closing the door and leaving me alone.

HOW'S IT BEEN GOING?

Seconds after entering the congenial gloom of Barney's Pub, I saw Dr. Frank Pearson, my former psychiatrist, sitting at the bar, waiting for me. A few weeks earlier, he had sent me a hand-written note, asking if I would meet with him on "a matter that would be of benefit to both our psyches." He specifically wanted to meet at Barney's because I had mentioned it so often and with such fondness during our sessions. I was taken aback. Didn't the shrinks' ethical code require that they wait to be called, like young women in the 1950s?

Our termination two years ago had been complicated. I had seen Dr. Pearson twice a week for three years. I went to see him because I was in the grip of severe depression, which was not a good thing for a lawyer who's in court a lot of the time. After a while I felt better and thought I had a pretty good grasp of the problem. I believed strongly that I was ready to have a go on my own, while Pearson thought there was still much to talk about. We discussed this for three months and couldn't agree. Finally, I self-terminated, which may be the coining of a phrase. After I stopped seeing him, my marriage issues, which had been simmering for a long time, finally boiled over. Martha and I got divorced. But generally I thought I had done well on my own. What would it prove to meet him?

So I didn't answer, but he sent a follow-up note. I kept thinking about his mention of benefit to both our psyches. Maybe there was something unresolved about the termination that needed to be discussed. I still didn't know what it would prove but decided to go along with it. If he wanted Barney's that was fine with me. I was fond of Barney's, a quirky place with the mandatory big TV screens that flash at you from all angles at all hours of the day, a long, shiny bar and a number of old wooden booths.

Barney himself does the cliché of the tough, tender-hearted bartender/listener one better. He is big, often loud and flamboyant, but no stranger to therapy himself. While he doesn't flaunt that fact, he is happy to have a discussion with you about his psyche or yours. So the talk at Barney's could as easily be about the id as the Red Sox.

I was almost cocky as the hour approached but my confidence drained the instant I stepped through the door. "Get out of here quick," I said to myself. Too late! Barney, red-faced and sweaty, waved one meaty hand at me and pointed with the other to Pearson. He knocked on the bar to get the doctor's attention, and pointed in my direction and yelled, "This guy's been waiting for you." Sometimes Barney is not so discreet. I wasn't exactly self-conscious, but by the same token, I didn't want to advertise this meeting. Anyway, at 4:30 on a Wednesday afternoon, the crowd was light. I walked toward the bar, managing to bump into a table en route, rattling the cutlery and causing Barney to sing out, "Way to go, Champ."

Pearson got up from the bar stool, and said, "Ben Hamlin, it's good to see you. Thanks for coming."

We shook hands and sat down on adjacent stools. Close up, he was not the distinguished looking psychiatrist I had seen for three years. He was a tall, thin man of about 60 years who, in the past, had always been trim and immaculately dressed. Now he looked simply gaunt. His shoulders slumped and graying hair curled around and over his ears. He wore a dark Brooks Brothers suit, that clothes unconscious as I am, I'm sure is one that he wore periodically during our time together. It was badly in need of pressing. His collar was open and his usual striped tie was askew. Seeing him like that made me feel uneasy.

Barney put a beer in front of me. Pearson, still nursing a scotch, declined Barney's offer of a refill. While this was happening, I checked the mirror behind Barney and could see our faces through the row of scotch, bourbon, gin, and Grey Goose vodka bottles that lined the counter at the back of the bar. Pearson loomed high over me, being about six foot three while I'm five foot six. I sat as tall as I could, to narrow the vertical gap. At forty-eight, I was comfortable for the most part with my still-black hair and a face that had nothing particularly classic about it but was okay. I liked the fact that I looked like someone who could get things done. I also favor the rumpled, tie askew look, so, for the first time, we shared a certain sartorial kinship.

Barney, who didn't have much to do at the moment, was edging closer, wiping down the already spotless bar and giving me an "Is this who I think it is?" look. I wasn't up to a three-way parley on the state of my psyche at the moment, so I shot a look at Barney, got up and said to Pearson, "Let's find a booth so we can relax and talk." I carried our drinks to a booth in the corner, and we slid in on opposite sides of the table. He laid a worn leather briefcase alongside him.

Our meeting began like an ordinary therapy session. He peered at me as if waiting for me to present him with a dream to interpret. After initially avoiding his eyes, (a force of habit from the old days when I was talking about something embarrassing), I treated him like a witness and looked back at him just as steadily. He turned away. We waited. I was determined to let him speak first, but did try to smooth the way a little by saying, "Have you been waiting long?"

"Not long." We continued to stare at each other and I noticed he was drinking very slowly.

Finally, he started. "How is your life, Ben? I have thought about you a lot. How are things with you and your father? I honestly thought you would be back to deal with some of those wounds that we opened and hadn't quite closed. But I guess I underestimated you, which is one of the reasons I'm here."

That was probably the longest consecutive string of words I'd ever heard from him. "Yeah, I've been getting along okay," I responded guardedly. "So why are we here?"

He looked away, avoiding my eyes. "We'll get to that in a little while, if it's all right with you. Let me just assure you that, while this meeting may seem a little bizarre, I have both of our interests at heart. I hope you'll see it that way."

Fidgeting with his glass, he went on. "But before I tell you why I'm here, I'd like to know more about your life right at the moment. That'll have some impact on what I say later." His look suggested that he expected me to say no, but he continued. "Is that all right?"

"Sure. I can do that. Things have been pretty good. My work has gone well. I'm a partner at the firm now. Plenty of my own clients. I still like the rough and tumble of the courtroom. On the personal front, Martha and I finally broke up last year for good, and we're in the process of getting a divorce. I think it's a positive step for both of us, and the kids seem to be adjusting okay. My father, I understand him better and keep my distance, which is the way I want it. He's in a nursing home. I go see him every week for an hour. He's pretty out of it." I was surprised to find myself choking up a little with that statement. "That's it in a nutshell. Bottom line, I don't regret stopping." I looked at him and paused before adding, "And I don't need another round of shrinking."

"A little defensive aren't we? Who said anything about more therapy?"

"Well, just now you said you were surprised I didn't reappear to close my wounds, as you called them."

"That was probably out of line. But it wasn't an invitation to more therapy."

Fair enough I thought. I don't need to be defensive. He's not here to rehash the past.

Pearson reached back to get a handkerchief from his pocket, and, in doing so, managed to knock a few peanuts from the bowl onto the table. He scooped them up in one hand and streamed them back into the bowl, looking embarrassed. Then, he wiped his face and put the handkerchief back. "Well, it sounds as if you worked things through about your father pretty well," he said. "And how are your relationships right now? There were some affairs as I remember, even during the time you were married."

"Come on, just one. Thanks for reminding me." What had happened to his incredible memory? "It was a serious relationship. It still could be. Her name is Millie. I just might marry her someday."

"That's great news, Ben," he said without much enthusiasm.

The after-work crowd was beginning to file in, heading for their favorite spots, ready to mull over the happenings of the day with the assistance of Barney's, "Name your poison." A few people waved at me and stared at Pearson. I waved back, trying to be friendly and not encourage visitors at the same time.

He paused and said, "Of course, I'm not saying anything about more therapy."

"Okay, that's me in a nutshell." It was time to press ahead, get to the heart of the matter. "Now can you tell me why we're here?"

He sat silently. I could see the lines on his face. He looked much older and vulnerable. I squirmed a little. This meeting wasn't going along party lines at all.

I tried to soften things. "Dr. Pearson, I have to say you look different. You're still looking good but not quite as natty as you were. What's going on?"

He had been sitting with his elbows on the table, rubbing the still half full glass with his hands. He put the glass down and sat all the way back in the booth.

"This is hard to talk about, but here's what happening. I haven't practiced for about a year. I reached the point I was so burned out I couldn't take another day of listening to people talking about their problems and having to nod and be sympathetic. Well, 'burned out' isn't maybe the right word." He paused. "Let's try 'bored.'"

I had my own image of him listening and nodding at the beginning of a session, and still listening and still nodding forty-five minutes later, eight hours a day. I could see how that could wear you down. But, anyway, he chose his profession.

"That's a great thing to tell an ex-patient. That his gut-wrenching revelations put you to sleep." I winced. "Sorry. I couldn't help that."

He nodded that it was okay.

Barney came over and put down another beer for me. Pearson gestured that he didn't want another scotch. Whatever his issue was, and I knew there was one, it didn't seem related to alcohol.

"So you just quit like that? What about all your patients who needed you?"

"Look, why should everyone rely on me? Who cares about me and my problems? I know that sounds awful, but that's the way I got to feeling."

I didn't like the look of self-pity on his face. "You sound like you want some sympathy from me." I leaned back and raised my eyebrows in a way I hoped was quizzical. "I almost feel like we're playing a game here." He looked hurt and distressed. The man really was in some kind of trouble, so I took the kind of chance I would never take in a cross-examination.

"I'm not sure what this is all about, but I'm going to jump in with both feet here. I know you're in some difficulty. But I don't think I've got the whole story yet." Without pausing, I forged ahead. "Right off the top of my head, I don't think you got bored. I think you cared so much and took your patients' problems so seriously that you felt a sense of personal responsibility for every patient who didn't walk out of your office with a shiny new ego. I think you just couldn't take the weight of other people's troubles any longer and felt you had failed."

I looked at him across the table. He was listening intently.

"Now listen, Frank, maybe you got bored a little. But, mostly, I think you were overwhelmed by your limitations, by the limitations that apply to anyone who takes on a healing role." I stopped, amazed at what had just come out of my mouth.

"You should have been a psychiatrist, Ben."

"Not on your life!"

After that summation, I thought I'd better shut up for a minute. We needed a break, and I thought of food. "I'm going to have a bowl of minestrone and the one-pound cheeseburger with bacon. And another Sam Adams. How about you?"

He shook his head. "What you said was pretty high-flown but there was some truth in your interpretation." He made a quote sign in the air around the last word. "Here's what really happened." He raised his right hand. "This is the honest-to-God truth. Yes, it was a lot more than getting bored. I had all these people for years and years dropping their problems in my lap in confidence. I took them on, oh, Lord, how I took those problems on, my noble mission." He looked sheepish. "Pardon me for the grandiloquence. But I really felt like I was doing something worthwhile. For a long time I was sure I was helping people. About a year ago, I found I just couldn't process any more problems. They kept accumulating inside me. I couldn't find a way to vent and get back to myself. I was stuck."

That's pretty unusual I thought, but I could understand it. I found myself growing sympathetic, reached over and put my hand on his arm. "Frank, that must have felt like hell."

"Yeah, it did. About the only good thing was that it gave me a new appreciation of how my patients, some of them, must have felt when they couldn't throw off a problem, no matter how hard they tried."

"I have to say from my ego standpoint, it's kind of nice to know your psychiatrist doesn't forget you the minute you walk out the office door." Again I couldn't stop a wisecrack.

He winced.

"I apologize, Frank. That wasn't very helpful. So what did you do?"

"I had to quit. It was sad because there were patients with real problems, but I couldn't help them any longer. Now, I'm seeing the doctor who trained me initially, Rudolph Stein, to try to get to the bottom of it. We're talking about counter-transferences, masochism, conflicts about helping and wanting to be helped, that sort of thing. Just talking about it is good. But I've got a way to go yet.

"That seems like a natural move. Should be no surprise to a psychiatrist that talking helps." I leaned back and had some other associations but I let them go. Take it slow I said to myself.

"Frank, is there something I can do here? Some way I can help you with this?" I could sense we were headed there, but I had no idea what form that help might take. He was my psychiatrist. I wasn't his and, yet, my response seemed almost automatic.

"That's it, Ben." He gave me an appreciative look. "I've been testing you out here, pushing your buttons, as they say, to see if you'd walk out before I proposed it. But so far, you're staying with me."

"Maybe I'll hate myself in the morning."

"Here's what Dr. Stein and I have come up with. I simply took on too much myself and didn't expect enough from my patients. I became disillusioned about how many really got better and figured that they wouldn't have the strength to handle the truth on their own. So I'd get obsessed with having to think about their problems. It was crazy, but I felt if I didn't keep doing that, my patients would suffer."

He stopped to see if I was following him. I wasn't at all sure—this was pretty confusing—but I nodded for him to go ahead.

"Ben, I'm seeing you because you were one that I worried about a lot. Now I can see that I didn't need to. Dr. Stein helped me with that. You were pretty tough and I just didn't give you enough credit. You wanted to terminate, and I told you I didn't think you were ready. Maybe you were, maybe you weren't, but it was ultimately your responsibility to make that decision. And I should have supported you, not tried to hold you back."

I started to speak but he held up his hand. "Here's the real reason I'm here today. I want to put you and your problems behind me. I'm hoping that I can give you back what I took on from you and have been carrying around for a long time. I think this will be a start toward liberation. You're the first one I've seen." He looked at me to see my reaction. I tried to keep a neutral appearance. He went on, appealing to me for confirmation. "This may sound crazy. But it feels right!"

He opened his briefcase, reached inside and pulled out a large brown envelope, stuffed to capacity. This does sound crazy, I thought. He put the envelope on the table. "I've written down a summary of the problems we wrestled with and, also, included all the notes I kept of our sessions. Things that I thought I had to carry around for you. I'm asking that you take back these problems." He smiled, anticipating one objection that automatically was on the tip of my tongue. "You're a lawyer. Yes, I know I'm supposed to hold onto my records." He shrugged that detail away. "How many people have a chance to help out their psychiatrist?"

He pushed the envelope across the table. I nodded but didn't pick it up. I knew I would have other reactions later, but I felt that I had to offer him more support.

"Frank, since you're a little down, I think it's only fair to tell you, absolutely sincerely, I always thought you were a pretty decent guy, even if you were a little stiff sometimes. You helped me a lot. Give yourself some credit."

"Thanks for all of that. I'm probably overcompensating right now but I think I'll get it right."

"I'm sure you will."

Pearson stood up. "Time for me to go." He glanced at his watch. It was the same gold Rolex he used to consult discreetly as the end of my hour approached. "I'm due at Dr. Stein's office." He looked at me and smiled. "Ben, I feel a little relieved. I hope this hasn't sounded too weird. Thanks for listening to me."

He looked down at the envelope. "I hope you'll be able to take that with you."

I picked up the envelope, waved it in the air as a salute to its significance, and then pushed and jammed to get it into my briefcase, which was full of files relating to an upcoming trial. He smiled gratefully.

We shook hands and both said, "Good luck," at the same time. He headed toward the door.

I knew that the minute he left, Barney would be over craving details. This was out of Barney's league. I had been given confidences that were not mine to divulge, so I left the pub as quickly as I could.

When I got home, I rummaged around in my briefcase, pulled out the now rather rumpled envelope, and, pushing aside a pile of magazines, gave it a clear spot on the coffee table. It was addressed to Benjamin J. Hamlin Esq., c/o Barney's Pub. I poured myself a scotch and sat down. As the scotch seeped through my system, I realized how tired I was and how stressed and difficult our meeting had been. Frank Pearson had turned the whole world topsy-turvy in the course of an hour. Talk about role reversal.

I had my feet up on the table and pushed with them at the envelope. Who asked him to bury my life so deep in his psyche he had to dig it out and hand it back to me, to cure himself? I had been doing fine until he came along. What the hell? Where was the famous "mutual benefit to both our psyches"? This train of thought was getting me confused and a little pissed at him.

I took one more scotch and softened a bit. Yeah, I had to feel sorry for him. He was a man in pain. But what could I do, what should I do, if anything, to help him? He had Dr. Stein. I was going to trust him on that. I jumped through a whole lot of unsatisfying mental hoops trying to make sense of it all. Finally I gave up the logical approach, partly because I was getting pretty drunk. I needed a clearer head. I went into the kitchen and poured the last of my scotch down the drain. Then, I fixed myself a ham and cheese sandwich. I drank two large glasses of cold water and stuck my head under the kitchen faucet until my head and my shirt collar were soaking.

Back in the living room, I picked up the envelope and took it to my desk. Taking a pen, I wrote underneath my name on the front of the envelope, "To whom it may concern: Delivery accepted. Contents not read. Anything herein may be considered in the public domain. I take full responsibility for the life described in these notes, one that was ended two years ago. In consideration of his work with me over a three-year period, Dr. Frank Pearson is released from any further responsibility for my life. In consideration of my taking my life back from him, I am released from any further responsibility for his life. Signed, Benjamin J. Hamlin, Esq."

I walked out of my condo and went to the trash chute, opened it, and unhesitatingly let my psychic life fall into the darkness.

Did I need to tell him what I had done? I didn't think there was any way to tell him the story without getting him all wrapped in me again. Maybe he felt a rush of air wherever he was and had a sense of something lifting off his shoulders as the envelope plummeted down the chute. In any case, he had given me the envelope and had not asked for an accounting. It was enough that I took it and listened to him seriously. It would have to be enough because that's really all I could do.

AN UNUSUAL SEASON

S am Stevens had made the Belton High varsity team as a freshman. He stood at shortstop in his brand-new uniform. It was the first game of the season, April 5, 1947.

Sam knew he looked pretty sharp, but, looks aside, he was nervous. Not just ordinary nervous, like Coach Haynes said you could expect to be, with sweaty hands or a lump in your stomach. Coach said that would go away quickly once the game started. Sam's problem wasn't a lump in his stomach. He wasn't sure what it was. He did what he could to get confident: shifted back and forth in a hunched over position like the pros did; spat in his glove twice; yelled stuff like, "No hitter up there," or "Easy out," in the pitcher's direction; and finished by patting the 1946 Ted Williams baseball card in his pocket.

Warm-ups finished. The plate umpire adjusted his chest pad. "Batter up." The lead-off hitter stepped into the batter's box. The catcher squatted down and signaled for a fastball. The game was on.

Sam was tested early by a sharp grounder well to his left, but he moved on it nicely, scooped it cleanly, and fired to first. Coach Haynes yelled, "Good work, Sam." Sam gave a sigh of relief. He hoped he'd stop being nervous. He had no further chances in the first.

In the second inning Sam found himself having trouble concentrating on the game. His nervousness was not contracting but expanding into a big balloon. His attempts to talk it up sounded as if they were coming from a tunnel, breaking into smaller and smaller bits until they just stopped.

Suddenly a bunch of the weirdest thoughts roared out of that same tunnel. His mind demanded to know what would happen if he suddenly focused on how, in detail, he actually fielded a ground ball, really focused on each individual move: how his body knew which way to move and how fast, when to bend over, when to cup the glove, when to scoop up the ball, when to squeeze it tight.

Having asked how he could do all of these complicated things that needed to be done all at once, his mind gave him a bad answer: If he thought about that, he would make a complete mess of the play.

He was thankful that nothing came his way in the second inning.

In the third, his mind continued its prosecution by forcing him to go through all the stages of throwing the ball, assuming he was able to pick it up. Sam felt he'd better check and cocked his arm for a pretend throw when a ground ball suddenly appeared before him. He was stuck with his arm up in the air. All he could do was watch the ball dribble into left field. The gasp from the crowd went right through him.

Before this disaster had registered fully, the next batter hit a grounder straight at him, a double play ball if there ever was one, begging to be scooped up easy as you pleased. He managed to oblige the scooping part with only a small bobble. Billy, the second baseman, was covering the bag, yelling "Throw it, Sam. Just throw it."

"Sam, Sam, don't wait too long," his mind exhorted him. "Don't hold the ball, Sam. Make sure you aim straight. Sam, you're going to screw this up. Throw it; No, hold it; no, throw it; throw it."

All that was required was a short underhand lob to Billy for a force play. But the ball just dropped from his hand to the ground and took two humiliating bounces en route to Billy. Both runners were safe. The crowd groaned loudly. Coach Haynes stood on the sideline, hands on hips, saying nothing.

Fortunately, the next two hitters struck out. When Sam got to the bench, Coach Haynes asked, "What happened? Are you okay?"

Sam mumbled, "I don't know. I don't feel so good."

Coach Haynes looked a bit relieved to have an excuse and said, "Okay, Sam, better take a breather."

Sam spent the rest of the game staring off into space. Coach Haynes didn't put him back in the game. When it was over he ran off the field, hiding tears, and went straight home.

"This will go away. Pull yourself together," Sam said to himself on the way home. He tried to sing "A Mighty Fortress Is Our God," a hymn his father had loved when he was alive, but the hymn drowned in his humiliating thoughts. So he whistled and tried to think about something else. The persistent vision of his pathetic throw hippity-hopping toward Billy wouldn't leave him alone.

Usually, when Sam got home, he went to the kitchen and got something to eat and drank a big glass of cold milk. This time he went straight up to his room and flopped onto his bed. His life was ruined. He had betrayed himself. Where had that crazy stuff in his head come from?

When his mother came home, Sam told her he didn't feel well and didn't want any supper. She hadn't been able to get to the game and was anxious to know what had happened. All Sam would say was he'd messed up really badly. She brought him some soup, but he could barely eat any of it. He skipped his usual evening practice of checking himself in the mirror to see if he could find any zits on his face and crawled under the covers.

He was awake most of the night, reliving the nightmare of the day. Nothing like this had happened to him before. He remembered a couple of times during a test exam when his head started telling him all kinds of things to confuse him. He got good grades anyway and hadn't thought much about that since.

The only other thing Sam could remember was actually sort of an experiment. He was looking in the mirror and saw himself blinking. Sam thought it was pretty weird that your eyelids opened and shut all the time and you never noticed. Then he wondered what would happen if you tried to catch yourself blinking. Would that screw something up somewhere? He forgot about that pretty soon, too

There was a big difference between the baseball disaster that happened in broad daylight and that other stuff. Nobody knew what was going on his head during the exam or when he was looking in the mirror and blinking away, but, when ground balls are rolling between your legs, everybody can see how you're screwing up. It feels like some gremlin had crept inside me and was making me do that, Sam thought.

At breakfast, he asked his mother to call Coach Haynes and say he didn't feel well enough to go to practice, but he told her he'd go to school. He was a very good student, (he'd actually skipped a grade), and he liked school a lot, but when he got there had to drag himself from class to class.

Coach Haynes found him after his last class.

"What's this I hear from your mother? You're not feeling good? C'mon, Sam. So you had some problems yesterday. You gotta get back on the horse after you've fallen off, right? Can't let it get the best of you, kid."

He started to give Sam a hearty slap on the back. When he saw his face, he patted him on the shoulder instead.

"Listen, maybe go home today and rest up."

He pointed a finger at Sam like Uncle Sam did in the war posters when he was making a personal pitch just to you to help win World War II.

"But you come tomorrow. We'll work you back in slow."

The next day Coach Haynes put Sam back at shortstop. The first ball that came his way was a moderately difficult ball he should have handled easily enough. By the time he got the glove in position the ball was long since by him. The same thing happened with another chance later in the inning.

This time when Sam came in from the field he actually yelled at Coach Haynes, "I told you I didn't feel good," and kept on going. Coach Haynes didn't try to stop him.

Fielding had been his thing. Sam felt comfortable about it. Several people had told him he was a natural. His hitting wasn't as good, but Coach Haynes had told Sam he had potential as a hitter. "You connect with the ball, but you need more power. What are you, a little over thirteen? God, you're already about 5'10" and weigh what, maybe 130 pounds? You'll fill out pretty soon. We're going to get your hitting as good as your fielding."

That made Sam feel great, and he was looking forward to his career taking off but he knew now that would never happen. He and baseball were through. When he got home he put the Ted Williams baseball card in his bureau underneath the clean underwear and socks.

Sam's sad mood continued. His mother wanted to help but there didn't seem to be anything she could do to make him feel better. Sam's father had died in World War II, so she had no partner or helpmate for support.

She did go to see Doc Burns.

"I'm so worried," she said. "He won't tell me anything. You know, he has gotten down sometimes; he thinks a lot, but this is the worst. I don't know how to help him."

"You're right. Sam's always been a sensitive kid. I think he's probably pretty anxious about making the team and got nervous. He's young and has a lot of growing to do, and I'm sure he misses his father. A boy his age really needs his father to help grow up."

He looked at her reassuringly and added, "If he'll come see me I would be glad to give him a quick checkup and talk to him. But, you know, this will probably go away on its own."

Sam knew how worried his mother was about him. He wished he could say something to make her feel better, but he just couldn't think of a way to tell her anything real. It was so embarrassing and weird. But, finally, he did think of a way to tell her at least something.

"Remember that story we used to read about the centipede who walked around so smooth with a hundred legs? And the jealous frog said that was so great and how did the centipede do it? The centipede thought about it and tried to figure it out and pretty soon he was all screwed up, flopped on his back with all his feet up in the air and was pissed, ahh, I mean angry, at the frog. The centipede never walked right again."

"Sam, of course I remember. We'd laugh over the picture of the centipede with its legs waving around. You said you felt sorry for the centipede. Hey, that's just a funny old story.

"Sam, yeah, I remember the centipede and how much you liked the story. I was just thinking the other day about what you liked, how much you loved King Arthur and Sir Lancelot and the Round Table and the heroic stuff they did. When you were seven or so you'd pretend to be Sir Lancelot and ride around the house on your little wooden pony waving a plastic sword with a funny helmet with a visor jammed down on your head. That was so cute."

She laughed. "You had a great imagination."

She went on, "Getting messed up like that doesn't happen to centipedes or anybody else. This will all work out before you know it. Just try to go on about your life and forget about what's over and done with.

His mother stood up and came around to his side of the table.

"I've talked to Doc Burns and he'd like to see you just to check and make sure you haven't got any medical problem."

Sam grimaced.

She bent over and kissed him on the top of the head. "I knew you'd do that. I know my son pretty well."

Back in his room Sam thought about how easy it was to invent the evil knights he fought and wished that there was something like that now he could fight against.

As for his friends, they didn't talk about his collapse around him except to say every now and then, "Hey, you're not feeling so good, so what do you expect? You'll be okay soon." Stuff like that. Sam knew that they were laughing at him behind his back. He thought of telling them he was getting Lou Gehrig's disease.

His friends did keep trying to get him to play ball with them. He wouldn't do it. He didn't do much of anything. Sam had always kept neat and clean. He'd used Vitalis and had his blond hair slicked back with a pompadour swirl or two in front that he thought the girls liked. Since the collapse he never washed his hair and seldom took a shower.

Finally, after a couple of weeks of doing nothing and being alone, he wandered out to one of the pickup games on a diamond on the other side of the playground from where the varsity team practiced. He watched for a while. Then, finally, he went out to play right field because there weren't many balls hit there and almost no ground balls, so there was less chance of screwing up.

Nothing much happened. Sam started playing, hoping nothing would come his way.

A week or so later, Sam noticed a kid about his age sort of skulking around in the patch of woods behind the field. He was pretty well-hidden, but Sam could see he was dressed in a faded green T-shirt, full of holes, and a pair of old jeans, also full of holes. Sam wasn't sure he even had shoes on. Dark hair hung down in tangled bunches around his ears and neck. It looked like neither the kid nor his clothes had been washed for a while. Maybe he doesn't have a mother to take care of him, Sam thought. Maybe he's a gypsy.

He reminded Sam of poor kids in the Pathé News reels who were war orphans and had lost their parents. They wore hand-me-down clothes like that. There was a big difference though. Those war orphans didn't have enough to eat and their faces were sad and full of fear. This kid was thin but looked very strong. He also looked sure of himself and not at all embarrassed by the way he looked.

What really struck Sam were his eyes. They were blue like Sam's, except they were a much darker blue and were locked in on Sam. He never seemed to blink. When the kid looked at him, Sam thought it was like being stared at by Superman.

As the pickup game went on, Sam was, as usual, tense and waiting to make a mistake, but he could feel those eyes drilling into him giving him a weird feeling of strength.

Next time he was up, he let the first pitch go and stepped out of the batter's box briefly. All of a sudden, he felt loose and easy, like he could hit the ball a mile. The next pitch floated up to the plate like a fat white balloon. Sam met the ball squarely and drove it between the center and left fielders. The ball rolled and rolled until it finally came to a stop at Coach Haynes's feet. The coach was way out in the varsity outfield watching the varsity practice. He picked up the ball and was waving it around, asking where he should throw it.

Their center fielder went over to Coach and the two of them had a short conversation. Then, they walked over to where Sam was. Coach Haynes tossed him the ball and said, "What's going on, Sam?"

Sam shrugged. "I don't know."

Then, he turned and looked for the kid. He was still there, way back in the woods staring at him without blinking, like a hypnotist.

They played another couple of innings, and Sam asked if he could play shortstop where he made two good plays and hit another home run as long as the first one. He could see Coach Haynes keeping an eye on their game.

When they finished, his friends crowded around him.

"Sam, what's going on, man?"

"Haynes is going to be after you."

His best friend, Bobby, came up to him and said, "You take a power pill or something? Let me feel those muscles." He grabbed Sam, who shoved him away.

"Cut it out," he said. "Hey, wise guy, did you see that kid hanging around the woods looking like a gypsy or something? Weird! I never saw him before."

"What the hell are you talking about?" asked Bobby. "What, are you seeing things? No one pays attention to our games. Why would they?"

He answered his own question with a shrug, then asked, "Are you okay?"

Sam nodded. He wanted the guys to go away so he could try to figure out what the hell was going on. When Sam looked again, the kid had vanished.

Sam felt great, although he had no idea what was going on. When he got home he dug his Ted Williams card out of the bureau drawer. While he was looking at the card, he all of a sudden decided to call the strange kid "the Kid," which was one of Ted's nicknames.

Coach Haynes wanted him as backup shortstop, so Sam showed up at practice the following Monday. It was mid-season. Belton was doing well so far but needed to win all of their remaining games to play for the championship.

As the week wore on, there was no sign of the Kid. Sam got worried. He still felt pretty strong even without the Kid around, but he could feel himself getting the jitters again. On Friday the Kid was back, just in time for the game, looking just about the same but maybe a little scruffier. He was lurking around again behind the trees way behind home plate a little farther back than before, staring hard at Sam.

Jack, the first-string shortstop, was sick, so Sam was starting. He hit a long home run plus a double that drove in two crucial runs. In the field, he was back to his old self. He was thinking mostly about the huge change in his hitting and not paying much attention to his fielding, which just seemed to take care of itself.

Coach Haynes was stroking his chin, looking both pleased and puzzled. When the game ended, the Kid had vanished again.

Jack the original shortstop turned out to be very sick and couldn't play the rest of the season, so Sam became the starting shortstop. He played really, really well as Belton won game after game.

Everybody was curious and wanted to know what was going on. "It's like a miracle" they kept saying, even his mother. Coach Haynes had his fingers crossed behind his back every time Sam went to bat.

All Sam could do was to shrug and say, "Maybe it is a miracle. I don't know what's happened. Hey, I feel good. It's no big deal. Things just clicked all of a sudden."

He actually liked to act nonchalant about it, like it was no big deal. He'd even have fantasies sometimes that it was him doing all the terrific hitting without any help.

But it was a big deal, and Sam tried not to think too much about what was going for fear of jinxing himself. His mother was happy but kept trying to find out what had happened to him. She said she wanted to understand so she could help him more.

Doc Burns told people, "I said he'd pull out of it."

The Kid wasn't around for practice for the most part, but even though he was sometimes late he made it to all the games. With each game the Kid was continuing to move farther and farther back in the woods and seemed to be getting more and more scruffy looking. His staring was still providing lots of power, but Sam thought his eyes were not quite so Superman-like as they had been.

Sam had resumed his good personal habits and sometimes when he looked at the Kid found himself thinking that he was really too scruffy. Then, he'd get guilty and mumble an apology in the Kid's direction.

For the final game of the regular season at the Belton home field, the Kid was there, way back in the woods. Sam hit a double and a single. Then with runners on second and third, he saved a certain two runs in the fifth inning with a spectacular play. The last time he batted, Sam connected well but the center fielder was able to catch the ball. Sam was surprised, because he felt like he hit it as hard as he could. Anyway, Belton was way ahead, so it didn't make any difference in the result.

The championship game was against Avery High on their field. As usual, the Kid hadn't attended practice, but as the game started he was still nowhere to be seen. If the Kid is gone, Sam thought, I don't know what's going to happen. He was nervous just like before the first game.

Avery had the fastest pitcher in the whole division, a cocky fourteen year-old named Hurley who was already six feet tall and looked sixteen or seventeen. Hurley had let his red hair grow long, and it stuck straight out from under his cap in all directions, as if it were oiled or just hadn't been washed in weeks.

His eyebrows were weird too. They were the same red color, started high up on the side of his head and then angled down sharply toward the bridge of a nose that was long and pointed. He looked like Batman's bitter enemy, the Joker.

Hurley liked intimidating batters by looking at them long and hard as they waited for his fastball to zoom over the plate. The first time Sam came up to bat, his mind, without the Kid around, was playing a trick or two about when to swing.

Hurley yelled at him rudely, "You're supposed to be a hot shot. You've never seen fast until now, kid. No more cheap hits for you," and gave him a long stare.

Five pitches later, Sam was out on a swinging strike three and Hurley turned a thumbs-down in Sam's direction, laughing as he did. Sam threw his bat down and went back to the bench. Coach Haynes came over and said, "That's okay, Sam. He's really fast. Don't feel you have to be aggressive. Just meet the ball."

Sam nodded. I didn't really think my way out of that. He just threw it by me. He was angry with himself, but he was angry with Hurley, too. Who does he think he is with all that stuff?

The next time up was somewhat better. Sam got his bat on the third pitch, holding back a bit as Coach Haynes had suggested, and hit it with some authority but straight at the shortstop. Back on the bench he checked for the Kid, sure, even before he looked, that he wasn't there. He was gone for good.

Coach Haynes said, "You're on to him now, Sam." Sam knew the team was waiting for him to break loose.

The score was tied one to one at the end of the sixth inning. Only one more inning to go.

He hadn't done anything at bat, but Sam had been really good at shortstop. In the bottom of the sixth, on one of those "no time to think" shots off Hurley's bat, he knocked the ball down after leaping high in the air and had thrown Hurley out easily, permitting himself a thumbs up and a small sneer in Hurley's direction. That had sort of evened things up.

In the bottom of the sixth, Hurley got the first two outs fast but then walked the next batter on four pitches. Sam was up. The walk looked almost deliberate to Sam, like Hurley wanted to pitch to him.

Sam stepped in. Hurley stared at him. Sam waved at him as if to say just quit that. Hurley fooled him with a changeup on the first pitch. He swung so hard he spun around and lost his balance.

"Easy! Easy!" Coach Haynes cut through the shouts and yells from both sides.

Sam decided to try something. When Hurley was finally ready to pitch, he backed out of the batter's box and the ump yelled, "Time." Sam did his best to stare right back at Hurley like the Kid would have done, trying not to blink. It was not a very good imitation tactic, but it was something.

Hurley's next two pitches were balls. With the count two and one, Hurley took his time and then fired a pitch that was the fastest yet. Sam held back for just a fraction of a second and then came around, making solid contact with the ball. It wasn't home-run quality, but it was good enough. The ball went shooting by the second baseman into right center. The base runner was around second in a flash, but the coach at third held him up.

The Belton season peaked there. Hurley struck out the next batter. In the bottom of the seventh Avery got a run, no thanks to Hurley. The championship was Avery's.

The loss was tough to take. The guys walked around looking very sad, saying, "Nice game," and, "We almost had it."

Coach Haynes slapped Sam on the back and said, "We had a good season." Sam could tell he was very disappointed.

Sam didn't want to talk to anybody. He had let the team down. One of those mighty home runs he had hit earlier in the season would have won the championship. He felt really badly.

Coach Haynes was busy talking to the others trying to make them feel better. "Wait until next year," and that sort of talk. Then he came over to Sam again.

"Your hitting was amazing for a while there. I don't know what happened. You lost some of that oomph near the end. I've been watching. I think you developed some sort of hitch in your swing or something, so you lost some of that good power, wherever it came from."

Sam shrugged. He couldn't look at Coach Haynes.

Coach Haynes wasn't through talking.

"Sam, I think I told you before that you had the potential to be a good hitter. Well, you turned out to be one quicker than I expected. Anyway, I want to work with you on your swing and get it back in the groove, see if we can get you more consistent."

He put his hands on Sam's shoulders and turned him so he could look him right in the eyes.

"That was a nice hit you got off Hurley at the end. We gonna work together a lot early next season. Let's see what we can do for you and for Belton. What do you think?"

Sam said, without a lot of enthusiasm, "Yeah, that could be great. But I'm not sure I can do what I did again."

"Of course, you can," said Coach Haynes.

He slapped Sam on the back again and turned and walked off because someone was calling his name.

A TIME IN THE LIFE OF ALBERT "Y"

PART I

On a warm October afternoon, shortly after my arrival in Paris, I was reading *Madame Bovary* when suddenly I noted a numbness developing in my left hand. I tried in vain to shake some feeling back into the hand. Perplexed, I returned to my studies, picking up a different text that required attention. Surprisingly, *Le Rouge et le Noir,* chronicling the amorous and ambitious adventures of Julian Sorel, restored normalcy. I could wiggle my fingers again and was deeply grateful for the ability to do so. The whole incident lasted no more than two minutes.

It was the fall of 1909. I had been at L'Institut in Paris for only a month, arriving from a small town in southern France. I was twenty years of age, innocent and full of a passionate desire to acquire the broadest and deepest levels of knowledge. I had no time for foolish interruptions and determined to ignore the strange happening.

Two days later, I experienced the numbness again. I awkwardly took up *Le Rouge et le Noir*, but this time the proffered antidote was summarily rejected. I wondered if it was significant that it was the right hand this time, and not the left, that was afflicted. I put down the Stendhal and went to my chemistry studies. Soon the right hand seemed relieved, but my left hand commenced a frightful nagging, as if resentful at being neglected. I reverted to *The Red and the Black*, which placated that demanding extremity once again. And so I went on for some time, alternating between Avogadro's number and Stendhal until full equilibrium was restored.

A truce went into effect for the next few days. I began to understand that the hand, whether left or right, hungered to receive nourishment that could be derived only from ingestion of a very specific sort of knowledge. Then, yet another episode occurred. This time the numbness extended from the fingers up to the elbows of each arm, first on the right and then the left as I alternated remedies. Fortunately, the diverse nature of my studies provides a variety of "food" between the sides. The addition of Pascal's Pensées and the periodic table to my literary diet had an appropriately calming influence.

I wanted to view this disturbance as an intellectual challenge. Why, indeed, were my arms choosing to interfere with this endeavor so critical to my well-being? Rationality would lead me to an answer.

For the moment I was living alone in a tiny room with grey walls, a scarred wooden desk, a hard chair, an even harder bed and a bleak view into a courtyard with one forlorn beech tree leaning crookedly to the left. There was a mirror somewhat bent with a long diagonal crack starting at the top right and angling down and left to a resting place slightly right of center. The mirror over time had achieved a certain concavity so, depending on my angle of view as I looked into the mirror, I was one of two very different looking persons. This became a bit of game I used to break the continuous cycle of study.

A few days later I made my first two friends: Bertrand and Francois, twin brothers, two years older than I. They, of course, looked quite similar, tall and black-haired with the swarthy complexions typical of their city of Montauban, except Francois had a slight scar on his lower right cheek. While their looks were similar, their academic interests were not. Bertrand was keenly interested in the poetry of the Symbolists while Francois had a bent for physics and talked a great deal about Albert Einstein. I felt initially shy with them, but their jovial ways soon put me at ease.

They introduced me to another student, Pierre "M," who was older, perhaps twenty-eight, in his third year of medical studies. He was a dauntingly thin person, tall and stooped with a face barely wide enough to accommodate all his features. His nose, too, was long and narrow and ended just short of a thick mustache and a beard that preserved the unities by narrowing to a point.

Pierre was carrying a heavy scholastic load with a particular passion for immunology. He talked slowly and with great precision, seldom laughing or joking. I would have thought him an unlikely companion for Bertrand and Francois, who wanted to enjoy a perpetual good time, but they were very respectful of Pierre and his wise ways. If I were to see him on the street, I would think him not a physician but an ascetic who had just arrived in Paris after contemplating the world in the Egyptian desert for ten years.

From the outset we shared a kindred seriousness. He said to me in the course of a conversation, "I am totally and completely committed to my career in immunology. I try to think of nothing else and to spend as little time as I can on other learning and other matters in general."

"Pierre," I exclaimed, "This is quite remarkable! My goal is the exact opposite. I want to learn everything about everything. I feel like I must."

I paused then, and said, "But I am frustrated right now."

I told him in detail what had happened to me recently and he listened with great interest.

When I had finished, Pierre looked at me and said, "Albert, I appreciate your trusting me. So your desire is to know everything, to be a human encyclopedia." He rubbed his beard vigorously. "Well, you are young and you want to be perfect. It's interesting. Many people with your energy and intelligence, I think, have a goal, want to put their knowledge to some use: make money, sing at the Paris Opera, help the natives in poor African countries."

I shrugged. "It's like a commandment that I embrace all learning."

"Speaking of embracing, what do you think is going on with your arms?"

I shrugged again. "I really have no idea but I am determined not to let it interfere."

"Albert, you have set yourself a daunting task indeed. Let me know if I can be of service."

We four soon made a practice of dining regularly together. Meal times were the only times when both Pierre and I could be persuaded to take leave of our books. I had shared my secret with Pierre already but was so charmed by the easy bonhomie of Bertrand and Francois that one night at the Café Bleu, I talked freely with them about my episodic symptoms. The twins listened attentively and were particularly fascinated with the fact that each side of the body had an appetite for a different sort of knowledge.

Bertrand began to giggle. He rose to his feet and announced, "It is our mission to help our dear friend, Albert, tame his unruly body parts. We must practice and prepare."

"Help Albert," the brothers chorused, raising their glasses to me.

Bertrand bent courteously close to my left elbow and asked, "You look a bit down. May I offer you a chapter of the *Iliad*, or would that be too hard to digest? Maybe, as an entrée after an hors d'oeuvre of Rimbaud."

Not to be outdone, Francois feigned panic, saying, "No! No! Bertrand, the real problem is a right scapula lacking knowledge of the theory of special relativity." He began addressing that shoulder blade and telling it about the speed of light.

They were consumed with laughter at their own wit. I was embarrassed but managed to laugh along with them. Every now and then, one of them would stop and say, "Albert, we are just being silly." When they finally stopped laughing, Bertrand put his hand on my shoulder and said with all apparent sincerity, "Albert, we really are your friends and will help you at any time in any way we can."

I noticed that Pierre did not join in the merriment and looked at me with sympathy, for which I was grateful. He studied me gravely while I was speaking. While I understood the prospects for levity in my situation, I did not want to play the fool.

Shortly after that, I had to prepare for both a chemistry and French literature exam on the same day. I slept poorly the night before, my head a jumble of formulae and phrases. After the exams were over, I returned to my room, very concerned about my performance, particularly in chemistry, where I had become confused at one point by an intrusion from the left side that insisted on thrusting into my consciousness the color of Madame Bovary's dress on the eve of her first infidelity, a point that would have been apt an hour earlier in my literature test.

Shortly after I sat down, my right arm began to tingle ominously and a massive attack of numbness developed. I attempted to pick up *On the Origin of the Species*, but, since my right hand was useless, I could not keep the book open. The numbness invaded my left arm. I was under full siege.

For a moment I felt like some possessed peasant in medieval France, certain that I had devils thrashing about in my body. When I tried to stand, I lost my balance and toppled to the floor, making a considerable noise and knocking some books off a nearby table. Fortunately, I was unhurt but in a difficult state.

By the rarest good fortune, Bertrand and Francois happened to be just outside in the hall, about to pay me a visit. They heard the crash, rushed into the room and quickly hoisted me onto the bed. Francois picked up the Darwin, while shouting to Bertrand to pick up Racine's *Phaedre*. The silly game of a few nights previous at the Café Bleu proved to be an excellent dress rehearsal for this darker drama.

The two began reading separately and slowly at first, so I could vaguely follow the H.M.S. Beagle's progress across the Pacific and the beginning of Phaedra's infatuation with Hippolytus. Then, they begin to read simultaneously at an accelerating pace, until their voices, rising and falling, blending and separating, sometimes sounded like the plainchants I used to hear at evening vespers in the company of my mother. The blur of sounds had the desired effect. I calmed down, fell asleep, and awoke feeling much better. No one was there. I am indebted to Francois and Bertrand, who were true to their word that they would help at any time.

I was now sufficiently disturbed to have a conversation with Pierre and see what course of action he would recommend.

"Albert," he said. "I am actually very sympathetic to your situation, as you know, and, well, to be frank, professionally fascinated. I see this at its root, as an immunology matter."

He paused, but only briefly. I had the sense that he was prepared for my request.

"I think we must exercise more vigor here because your adversary is very determined. I have a theory that viruses are fiendishly clever in finding ways to circumvent solutions the body puts up and new vaccines will need to be found to curb them. Not yet proven. Anyway, my thought is that, perhaps, that this may be happening in your case. Remember the demands the other night came from both arms at once, a more complicated scenario." He paused for some response.

I said, simply, "Please go on, Pierre."

"I have given your, ahem, problem more than a bit of thought. I know that you have been creative in findings ways of countering these unusual phenomena, using materials from your courses."

He warmed to his subject, stroking his beard frequently.

"But I think more system is needed. I would make books available on a preventative basis. In other words, and in brief, instead of randomly trying to counter an attack with a volume you have at hand, I could prepare charts that will provide antidotes, an appropriate immunity before you start your study. We will have those antidotes ready at all times. If conscientiously taken, they will prevent these attacks of yours."

He paused. "What do you think?"

While I grasped the concept of immunization well enough, it was a bit hard for me to see its application to my case. I wondered how increasing the heavy load of reading I already had could help. But I could see how excited he was at his plan and knew he would be hurt if I refused. Pierre is a friend, I said to myself, and he will very soon be a doctor. I will trust him.

Once unleashed, Pierre was unflagging in his dedication. He vastly expanded the antidotal inventory by compiling lengthy lists of all the giants of literature from Homer to Ibsen and the great personages of mathematics and science from Archimedes to Einstein. He also convinced an artist friend to make a detailed anatomical chart with arrows running from a particular body part to a box containing suggested readings to counter a specific paralysis and posted the chart over my bed. Pierre also visited me regularly to check on whether the lists and chart required amendment or addition.

I tried, with good intent, to carry the plan out, but it became clear very soon that this approach was not helping, and it did in fact interfere with the work I had to do. Pierre was concerned that I was not using adequate amounts of the antidotes and pressed me to persevere. I argued with him and, finally weary of that, I had to be untruthful, which I disliked. I was sorry I could no longer confide in him because I knew he wanted to be helpful, but I felt he had strayed from the path of reason.

As the time for semester exams drew near, I studied night and day, allowing myself a mere three hours of sleep. I sat surrounded by volumes of all sorts, not only those relevant to my preparation but those to which I was supposed to refer as antidotes. The later were stacked high against the walls of my room, as far away as I could place them and, still, be able to point them out as relevant when Pierre came for his regular visits.

I was reaching the point where I felt I was literally pushing knowledge into already overcrowded spaces inside me, as if I were a goose about to be measured and examined for the quality of its liver. My left and right sides, appearing to realize that I was running out of room to store the knowledge they required, accelerated their demands and competed ever more strenuously for preference.

I took the examinations and, somehow, managed to do extremely well. My professors noted with pleasure my academic excellence. I was hopeful that these positive results would bring me satisfaction and relieve some of my symptoms, but I noticed only a modest diminution and knew that I was reaching the bursting point.

Meanwhile, our dinner practice continued. As recess drew to a close, Bertrand said we should be more daring and adventurous in our nighttime activities. On the last Saturday night before classes resumed, we lingered longer at the table and had more than the usual amount of wine. Francois suggested casually that we visit Madame Bouvais's establishment.

At first I was shocked at the prospect. It would be my first time with a woman. Further this would be with a prostitute, a fallen woman as the Bible and the church viewed her. But, after yet more wine, I suddenly cried out, with a spirit that surprised me, "Yes, let's go. Bring on the girls." For most of the evening, symptoms of numbness had been strangely and pleasantly absent.

"That's our Albert," approved Francois. "We are going to Madame Bouvais's."

As we neared her establishment, my steps faltered. I was perspiring heavily. Numbness was developing in that area where I fervently wished for a quickening. I said as calmly as I could, "Gentlemen, I am having an attack and cannot proceed."

Pierre began groping in his book bag for an antidote, but Francois waved at him to stop and said to me, "My dear friend, don't be afraid. Madame will have the answer. There is nothing that Madame's unique knowledge and vast experience in this area cannot cure!"

I did not want to appear unmanly in front of my friends, so we continued on our way. Pierre said he could not join us, pleading a lack of money, but would remain outside. We ascended the stairs to the first floor and were quickly in a richly decorated salon, its dark red walls covered with numerous paintings showing buxom young women embracing handsome young men or being pursued by merry satyrs. A dozen lovely young women, wearing only short maroon robes fastened loosely at the waist, were standing about or sitting on plush red cushions. The robes hid little of their considerable charms. I remained in a very anxious state. Madame Bouvais, a tall, handsome woman, perhaps forty-five years old, elegantly dressed and heavily bejeweled and powdered, welcomed Bertrand and Francois with familiarity.

She gave me a look that was appraising and severe but, at the same time, seemed to find something appealing in my obvious anxiety. She asked me to choose first. I became redder than the cushions and could do nothing but stammer.

"Well, my shy scholar, I can tell this is your first time. Marie is just the one for a scholar like you. She is new to us, as innocent and fresh to the sport as you."

One of the loveliest of the young ladies, with black hair, the whitest skin imaginable, and a sweetly innocent face, detached from the group, took my hand and led me down the hall into a small reception area adjacent to a spacious and well-appointed bedroom. The walls of both rooms were covered with photographs and images of a highly erotic nature—men and women copulating in every conceivable fashion and, even, in some cases, with animals. I had read about Khajuraho a famous temple area in India, and asked if that was where the images were from. She confirmed that I was correct, blushing as she did so, and went on to tell me that Madame was a devout disciple of the Tantric school, a Tibetan Buddhist approach, holding that one achieved the highest plane of spirituality through ecstatic sexuality.

We both fell silent for a few minutes. She said to undress, which I did with her help, feeling self-conscious because I considered my body quite inadequate. She smiled and laughed quietly at my embarrassment and said, "You are a very pretty boy, Albert, and very white. Not like some of those hairy old men." Then, she helped me put on a white robe. She disrobed and stood, completely nude, a strange and wondrous sight to me.

My heart beat more rapidly. There were pleasant sensations in my loins, but I sensed incipient numbness in my hands and arms. Fortunately the novelty and excitement of the moment made it pass. She possessed a natural dignity that put me at ease. I told her I was a student and some details about my life. I even told her my name, although she smiled and tried to hush me when I did. Such honesty was apparently not appropriate behavior in a place like this. She politely declined any information about her background. Despite her unfortunate occupation, she impressed me as being educated and sensitive and, happily, gave every appearance of liking me.

Our conversation continued for several minutes without any physical contact. Then, she stood up, and said, "Shall we begin?" We stood up. With some urgency, I dropped my robe and we pressed closely together and, as one, moved toward the plush bed.

I blush even now with what followed and will not say anything further, except to make the observation that for a time I was in a very different state, far removed from the intellectual.

It was over all too quickly but, almost immediately, I was ready to repeat the experience, when there was a rap on the door followed by the voice of Madame Bouvais saying firmly, "Are you quite finished, my young scholar? No, of course not. I know how you young men are. Marie is irresistible, but even for you this first time the rule applies; only one moment of sweet delight or a thirty-minute period, whichever happens first. I am sure the former applies."

The ecstatic moments were over. I stood up and hastily put on my clothes.

"Please come again!" Marie said. "I wish you could stay." Then, she patted me and said, "You are such a nice boy."

As I opened the door I was suddenly seized with nausea; buffeted, pushed, and pulled about by the wildest feelings in my stomach, as if giant waves were breaking in all directions simultaneously. My body, that had been so gratified moments ago by a thrilling new experience with its blissful climax, was rebelling violently. I bypassed the startled Madame, waving her out of the way feebly and started down the stairs, at which point I lost all bodily control and went crashing downward, bouncing from side to side off the wall. I arrived at the bottom and tumbled into the street, knocking down Pierre who was waiting just outside the door. We helped each other up. I couldn't stand on my own.

At that instant, my mind became a violent battlefield. Sharp fragments of knowledge broke from their sources and tumbled about inside me like crazed followers of Dionysus looking for victims to tear asunder. There were jumbles of numbers and formulae, crazily colored sketches of finches with beaks of various sizes protruding from their tails, notes of music bent this way and that, topsy-turvy combinations of French, English, Latin, and Greek letters, meaningless bits of text from sources as different as Balzac and Job, all bumping and contending with each other. A thousand readings from a thousand disparate disciplines would have had no salutary impact.

This mad struggle went on for a time, increasing in intensity. Finally, there were no survivors.

Other images, which had been waiting on the periphery, began to migrate toward the center. There was a circle composed of soft creamy breasts, a row of lovely, erect nipples, shapes and curves of faceless young women, then exquisite female faces with no bodily attachment, bold images of both the male and female organs suffused with desire, even an image of Marie. Finally the entire revolving chaotic mass lost any recognizable parts and dissolved into long strands of colors, ranging in a full spectrum from the purest white and blackest black in passing and finally ending pianissimo, with a few wisps of color fading into a void. My vision à la Hieronymus Bosch had ended.

I remembered shaking hard and feeling a powerful heat throughout my body. I remained on my feet until it was over. As it ended, I could feel myself falling toward the pavement with Pierre trying to catch me.

PART II

When I regained consciousness it was morning. I was lying on my bed, my body sore and battered. The events of the last evening came back in small bits and pieces: the promise and realization of adventure, the thrill of my all too short time with Marie, the body's fall down the stairs and collapse, then the chaotic and terrifying vision. I looked at the books lying about on the floor with a total lack of interest. My arms were quiet. I felt completely empty, devoid of intellectual desire. That made me uneasy even as I was glad of some relief from the compulsion to learn.

I spent the next three days in my room, nursing body and soul. Pierre came by. I thanked him for taking care of me, but told him I didn't want to talk. He left me a note on the table that I didn't read for a time. Bertrand and Francois came by and stood outside in the hall, calling to me. It sounded as if they had been to a party. I started to respond and caught myself. I needed cheering up but had decided in the aftermath of the night at Madame Bou-vais's I didn't wish to see them. While they were truly helpful during one of my episodes, I could not abide the rather certain probability of their making fun of my current predicament. They knocked on the door several times and yelled, "Albert, we love you. Albert, we love you," in slurred tones, stopped, muttered something unintelligible, and walked away.

Listlessly, I dragged myself to my classes. I could not find in myself a will-ingness to restart the learning process. This loss of passion for the goal to which I had dedicated my life filled me with sadness. Nor was that sadness redeemed by my introduction to the world of sensuality. I reflected on my vision. It seemed that my intellectual sides had annihilated each other in their struggle and sensual images were in the ascendency at the vision's end. However, that realization brought no happiness or peace of mind

In his note Pierre said that he felt it was best for us to terminate our professional relationship, saying that he had been wrong to take on my treatment and recommended that I seek other help. "I realize it was hubris on my part to think I could help you. I am worried that there is more to come, particularly after your strange spell last night. I became more involved in your dilemma than I should have. For this I apologize. I have learned a valuable lesson about myself: I must focus only on my medical studies. I do hope we can maintain our cordial personal relationship. I sug-gest for the moment we not see each other unless you require companion-ship. I am happy to support you if I can."

He signed his note, "Your humbled friend."

I agreed with his analysis and suggestion about our relationship and wrote a note to him to that effect. At the same time I knew I would miss his genuine concern for my welfare.

Marie was much on my mind. As my bruises and body healed and my mind settled a little, I found the desire to be with Marie returning strongly. I would have wished that desire to be combined with a renewed joy in learning, but that was not occurring. It seemed to me the only course was to follow my instincts of the moment.

After some days, I returned eagerly, but not without some apprehension, to Madame Bouvais's. Without ceremony, that formidable woman sent me off with Marie.

"I was so concerned about your fall down the stairs," that very pretty person said.

She removed all of my clothes and then gave me a healing and pleasurable rub. I was without the early anxiety of the other evening and eager to proceed. The initial pleasure was over fast, but I was soon ready again. She wanted conversation, but I wanted only to continue loving her physically, which was giving rise to such amazing sensations.

I was deeply concerned about my arms. They remained uninvolved, but I was suspicious. Despite that, I became so insatiable for our unions that I felt I had to apologize for my eagerness. No Madame came to curtail our activities. Finally, Marie said, "You must go. I am tired." I said how much I liked her and was absolutely sincere.

Madame rose to greet me in the reception area. She was alone.

"My young scholar, I am only charging for one time tonight because of the unpleasant conclusion to your first evening here. But if you want this privilege in the future with darling Marie, we will have to discuss terms which I hope you will find satisfactory."

I was bewildered and wanted only to rest.

"Shall we do that now?"

"If you please, Madame Bouvais, on my next visit."

I returned the very next night to Madame's wanting to be with Marie once more. I must have looked a bit distraught because Madame Bouvais did not press me on terms.

Our first time that night continued the pattern of our previous nights. As we rested I was aware of some fatigue and a growing numbness in both arms. As we were commencing a second time, the numbness became complete. I was unable to hold Marie as I wanted to do. We were well along in the process and neither of us wanted to stop. The numbness above was counterpoint to an increased capacity below the waist. But, then, the reality had to be faced.

She said, "What's the matter, my dear? What's wrong? Is it something I have done? What may I do to help?"

I assured her she was the loveliest and finest of all women and that it was my strange problem. I told her a little about the way my arms fought over knowledge and said I would tell her more at our next meeting. My two arms now seemed to be in league together to thwart our pleasure, to make a judgment on my behavior. We continued on; my lower body did its part and more to try to make up for the rude behavior of the upper, but I felt helpless and sad. Although this was the first new manifestation of my malady, I knew for a certainty that there would be more such occurrences. I apologized many times before I left; I told her again and again it was my fault. She looked confused and hurt but told me it was all right. I wished I could have believed her.

Madame Bouvais attempted to stop me before I left but I was feeling quite dizzy and waved her away. Once again, she seemed to grasp my poor state and did not push. I gave a vague nod of thanks and then descended with only slightly better control than on the occasion of my first tumbling exit down those very steps.

My anxiety was even greater than with the conflicts over knowledge, worse in part because there was another person involved for whom I had fond feelings. Also, during the intellectual crisis I had, at least, been able to free up one side with my alternating remedies. Now both arms were numbed beyond use during the act. I was too embarrassed to return to Marie, as much as I liked her. I did not want to know what proposition Madame Bouvais had in mind.

How was I to deal with the challenge my arms had contrived? I had barely discovered a whole new world of experience before these bitter adversaries had formed an alliance and struck with a combined force. Looking back over my recent history in the intellectual arena, I wondered if the problem, again, could be one of a conflict over variety, pitting the literary against the scientific. Going through the numerous volumes in my room, I found *Madame Bovary* as well as *Le Rouge et le Noir* and the original chemistry text and read them out loud repeatedly. My arms refused to be fooled by this rather obvious attempt to restore them to their former adversarial position. Their avowed enemy was now beneath them, literally and metaphorically. They had become my inflexible moral guardians.

I tried, once more, to revive my intellectual interest by attending class but only succeeded in falling asleep. My professors, who had become accustomed to a bright and responsive student, at first gave me strange looks and then began to ignore me.

Francois had told me of Montmartre, where he said young women, intelligent and sensual, came nightly. By day they were students. They were believers in free love as a part of their education and, by night, were glad to bestow bodily favors without expecting compensation. Perhaps, there, in the shadow of Sacré Coeur, I could find healing variety.

I went to Montmartre and proceeded to Le Café Noir, which Francois had recommended. I had no sooner seated myself when a lovely young woman with jet-black hair and smooth olive skin approached my table, saying, "You are new here, are you not, monsieur?"

One thing quickly led to another. Her name was Naomi; like Pierre, she was studying to be a doctor. She put me quickly at ease, and we had wine and a pleasant conversation, after which she took me to a room she shared with another young woman named Beatrice who appeared as we were making love. That seemed not to disturb either woman. As soon as Naomi and I had commenced, my difficulty occurred and my arms froze. Naomi asked what was the matter, but my instinctual half took the lead with such authority that her questions soon ceased and she gave herself over to the moment.

Beatrice, a brunette of very pale complexion, watched us with amazement and asked if she could be with me. Naomi was exhausted and readily agreed to share. Beatrice was a psychologist and was fascinated by my problem. I explained my issues to them briefly and my hoped-for solution in Montmartre. I was soon ready again, eager to see if the contrast which was clear between the two women, both in appearance and field of intellectual interest, would be helpful. Alas, once again, the arms continued their static rebellion. I felt, as I had when I last left Marie, like a person split into two wholly irreconcilable parts.

My eccentric yet stimulating behavior made me instantly well-known in the district and variety was available to me in abundance. But the result was the same in each and every case. There was Mimi, a ravishing and rather plump woman whose hair was dyed blond; Terese, tall and willowy; Claire, a petite redhead; Gertrude, magnificent from Sweden; and Genevieve, a dark gypsy who said she was of Romanian extraction. The women were titillated by my unusual approach and quite pleased with my abilities, not knowing it was earned at such a cost to my wellbeing. They were looking for excitement and not affection, so my inability to embrace them did not seem an issue. I was very embarrassed as my lower parts went their mindless way while my arms wanted only to thwart any sort of pleasure. As I flailed away, paralyzed above, intensely alive below, I felt like a freak at a country fair.

After twelve days of this I was physically and emotionally exhausted and descended the butte of Montmartre, in worse condition than the day I had ascended.

PART III

For days I did not venture from my flat, living essentially as a hermit. I thought about looking up Pierre but decided against it. One night in Montmartre while I was with Genevieve, I believe, I met Francois, who was very drunk. He slurred his approval of my companion and expressed surprise that I had found such a beauty. I asked about Bertrand. His face darkened as he told me they had had a falling out over some aspect of their varying studies and had not spoken for some time. I thought as I looked at him that the sensual life had its definite pitfalls and was glad that I had been able to stay away from alcohol and stronger medicines.

Sitting among the shambles of my life, I took stock. I had made no progress in my attempts to break the ties that bound me literally and figuratively. I had not gone down to glorious defeat, proudly throwing down the gauntlet to fate and losing. I had been done in ignominiously by myself, by the blatant hostility of my own arms. Most gallingly, the hands with their opposable digits, evolution's ultimate glory, were rendered useless, unable to grip a book full of learning or hold a soft body.

During the next days I was very sour in mood and without a plan. I was exhausted but restless. I began taking walks along the quays past the dark, silent waters of the Seine, trying to calm my mind. My various body parts were so at odds, each with the other, that they caused me to lurch along in an ungainly manner. It was as if I was a poorly made machine that would not hold together much longer.

Often on these walks I would stop by the riverbank and watch the murky waters move sluggishly past me on their way toward the English Channel. At least the mindless river had a goal, a purpose, a direction that I lacked.

A few nights later I was walking past the Bouquinistes near Quai Voltaire. It was late and only a few vendors were still at their places. I felt a familiar force building inside and pulling me toward one bookstall in particular. I knew instantly my arms were trying to assert their old dominion and tried to resist. The bookseller was an old man with a pale face and skin so thin that the dim light seemed to penetrate to and illuminate the fragile bones of his face. He was small and had bushy black eyebrows criss-crossed with white hairs. I thought he looked like some ancient sage, ethereal in appearance. He rose from his stool as I neared the stall, turned without a word, and handed me a worn copy of *King Lear*.

I paid for *Lear* and tried to leave but was held in place as if by magnets, until I had purchased successively the complete poems of Mallarme and the *Odes* of Horace. The bookseller spoke never a word but unerringly picked out works that appealed to my literary side.

After those purchases, I was able to move away but felt a second powerful force pulling me forward, toward another stall a little further down the quay. At the same time, the first force reasserted itself so I was pulled in two directions at once. My upper body was leaning back in the direction of the first stall, while my legs were being pulled toward the second stall.

After a short time, the pull toward the second stall prevailed, my body straightened up, and I stumbled closer. The proprietor was a burly man of about fifty with a frown on his sallow face that seemed engraved there to thwart any desire he might have had to smile. His black hair was thinning on top, but its long, stringy locks fell below his shoulder blades. He wore a dirty blue smock with test tubes filled with strangely colored liquids and notes with scribbled formulas spilling from his pockets. I knew he was a man of rationality and science. As I was pulled nearer, he said, "I will save you from that purveyor of fallacies and myths. His books tell you nothing of how the world truly is. Only science understands."

Bound within his periphery, I had no choice but to buy two ponderous tomes to effect my release. This was not the end. As I was released from the pull of the science stall, I felt yet another powerful drag toward still a third stall. The proprietor was a woman, quite obese with coarse black hair and swollen red features. On her face there was a wart of considerable size, sprouting several long dark hairs. Despite her unappetizing appearance I sensed that she was once pretty and even now she moved with a certain gracefulness that belied her bulk.

"I saw where you were, and I know what those intellectual snobs gave you, the prigs."

She laughed, her body quivering obscenely. "I have just the thing to take care of those hypocrites. Here's *Pantaguel and Garganta* by that libertine scholar, Francois Rabelais. A man of great parts." She laughed again, uproariously, as she made a lunge for my crotch. She opened the Rabelais and pointed to a lewd woodcut of a peasant man and woman making love on top of a hay pile, his breeches around his ankles and her rough dress high above her thighs.

"Ah, my young beauty? That's where your heart is at the moment."

The gross lady tried to touch me again, and I pulled away. She gestured behind the bookstall where there was a worn blanket.

"Do it with me and you can have Rabelais for nothing and I'll give you the DeCameron as well."

She would not give up and seized hold of me, trying to drag me behind the bookstall and loosen my belt at the same time. I dropped the books and resisted strenuously. Out of the corner of my eye I saw the ethereal bookseller approaching. Outraged, he had found his thin, piping voice, and was squeaking,

"Harlot, release that man before you besmirch him with your filth."

He, too, took hold of me where there was space not already occupied by the immense arms of the woman and sought to pull me away. She held to me with one arm and, with the other, tried to disengage the bookseller, half her size but tenacious. She yelled at him, "Hypocrite, zealot, judge not that ye be not judged."

Not to be outdone, the man of science joined in the fray, screaming at the woman, "Whore of Babylon," and at his literary counterpart, "Mystic, obscurer of pure truth!"

The ethereal bookseller responded, "Bloodless creator of destructive weapons. Man of narrow vision."

Science had his own formidable strength and found a place where he could both encircle me and engage the others.

I rebelled at being in the midst of this grabbing and pawing and screamed at them to stop. Finally, I managed to extricate myself, striking at all of them alternately with a desperate strength. The unholy trio promptly fell upon each other with renewed vigor, howling in a most uncivilized way.

I wanted to flee that confounding place and, fled up the quay as fast as I could, but I couldn't resist the urge to see what was happening. I looked back and the three were still pummeling each other. I had the distinct sense that the disparate parts that had tormented me from within had suddenly materialized in the physical world. It was as if I had been turned inside out and that the struggle was for my very soul.

The two men joined together and attacked her. They fought on, an even match. Panting from their struggles, they stopped and eyed each other with hatred. After a short pause, the seller of science books lunged, not for her, but for her bookstall that he proceeded to drag with a miraculous strength, books and illustrations spilling this way and that, to the edge of the river. With a final push, he sent it out of sight. The woman, who had not moved during this, rushed to the literary stall. She gave a primitive scream as she picked up his entire stall and let it fly over the bank to join the first in a slow progress up the Seine. Then, together, she and the once-meek literary seller jettisoned the science stall.

It was not over. Like rutting animals, they resumed the struggle. Now it was science and literature pitted against sex. The two men strove mightily to push the woman ever closer to river's edge. Finally they were able to push her into the water and turned on each other, teetering on the brink of the river. Still fiercely grappling, their wretched bodies so entwined they were indistinguishable, they finally pitched over the edge into the Seine.

Without looking back I ran off aimlessly into the night. After much floundering about with wrong turns and all, I finally made my way home and staggered into my flat, totally exhausted. After some wine, I got into bed. My mind was so busy trying to sort out what happened that it was dawn before I fell asleep.

The next morning, weary but full of curiosity, I directed my steps to the Quai Voltaire. I had no idea what, if anything, I would find.

As I approached, I could see neither the rival vendors nor their stalls, nor any books. I walked slowly past the site, braced for the contrary magnetisms that had gripped me a short few hours before. There were numerous vendors, but no strange forces tugging at my body.

Perplexed, I continued up river. I walked a considerable distance until I reached a bucolic section of the Seine I was sure I had never seen before. No one was around. There was a clump of bushes near the river, and I lay down to rest.

After resting a while I stood up at the water's edge and soon found myself swinging my arms around in circles this way and that. Meanwhile my legs, on their own, started doing a funny little folk dance that I had learned as a child. When that stopped, I took off my shirt and shoes and, after checking to make sure no one was coming along the path, took off my trousers and stood there in my undergarments.

The water seemed much cleaner than the water downstream. The Seine was not supposed to be a healthy place to swim, and I myself had seen unsavory looking objects floating by. I shrugged off any concerns and, taking a deep breath, jumped into the cold water.

I swam out near the center and, after another big breath, dove below the surface. I forced myself down, down until it was quite dark and I was growing short of breath. Reversing course, I drove myself upward. As I neared the surface I could see the sunlight flickering across the water.

LESTER AND CROWN VIC

It was Friday March 16, 2008. Lester Frank left work on the stroke of five. He aggressively worked his way through the crowd on the corner of Bowery and Delancey and hailed a cab. The next day was Lester's 40th birthday. Everybody gets depressed when they turn 40, with the inevitable feeling of life passing you by and opportunities for true accomplishment fading. Lester was no exception. On top of that, he was having particular trouble with low self-esteem—more trouble than most, he thought, because of his size. He was just about five foot three and believed people looked down on him, not just literally, but figuratively too.

Lester gave the driver the address of a garage called CopEx in the Bushwick section of Brooklyn. He was on his way to buy himself a birthday present, which would set him on the path to rejuvenation. He was on his way to buy a 2006 Crown Victoria. Crown Vics, of course, had been for many years the vehicle of choice for police departments all over the country. The car is especially designed for the rigors of police life—ready to make quick stops with a squeal of brakes and swerve nosily around corners in hot pursuit with blue lights whirling and sirens wailing. Lester was buying a car that had an inherent authority and commanded universal respect.

The trip to Brooklyn was slow and expensive, the driver too talkative at first and then surly as they wandered through the dark streets. Eventually they arrived at the CopEx office, which was a small cinder-block building planted in the center of a large lot with Crown Vics of many colors fanning out in every direction, quietly awaiting a new master. A lonely light in the office was the only illumination. As Lester headed up the steps to the office, the door opened and out stepped a man who loomed high over him.

"Lester, I'd about given up on you," growled Sean, the owner.

"Sean, this place is a long way from Manhattan," Lester countered, waving a check. "Here's your certified check for seventy-five hundred dollars." He was pissed off that the height disparity, accentuated by the fact that he was on the lower step, meant he was looking straight at Sean's hairy gut, the man having emerged from the office without a jacket and with his shirt half unbuttoned. Slob, Lester thought.

Money in hand, Sean led the way into the lot after flipping on a series of lights that cast a kind of sickly yellowish glow over the cars. In the second row, he stopped in front of a four-door maroon sedan and kicked the left front tire twice by way of introduction.

"Here she is, Les, a real beauty, courtesy of NYPD, borough of Bronx. Worked one of the toughest areas in the whole goddamn country."

He draped a brawny arm over Lester's shoulders.

"She's like new! Runs like a dream. Purrs like a pussy. You'll love it! Guaranteed parts and labor for fourteen days. "

He paused and then said, as he handed him the keys and gave him a friendly punch in the left upper arm that hurt for the next hour, "And the driver's seat is pretty high up, so you won't need a cushion or anything."

Lester bridled at that and thought about returning the favor of the punch, making up for the height difference with a friendly hook to the gut, a punch that he had used to great advantage in his late teens when he was one of the better featherweights in Hartford, the land of Willie Pep, the best little boxer of them all. Then he had respect.

He weighed the possible causes of Sean's action and remark and the consequences of reciprocity and decided Sean probably was trying to be nice in his stupid way and wouldn't consider such moves on Lester's part appropriate. Before taking off, he lowered the window partly and announced, "Tomorrow is my fortieth birthday."

Sean, with the transaction concluded, gave an indifferent wave and walked back toward the office, at which point Lester, still a little hot, offered a middle digit to Sean's retreating back, making sure he kept the gesture well below window height.

Lester was a little rusty but had been, when younger, a skillful driver. During the summers when he was fourteen and fifteen, Lester had spent a lot of time at his uncle's farm in northwestern Connecticut. There was an old Ford Pinto rusting in a barn. His uncle let him drive around the property to his heart's content and taught him a few stunts. Lester would go out on the back roads and practice swerves and complete 360s. He loved to do that. When he was in his teens, he and his friends would race noisily around the country roads outside Middletown, Connecticut, in old cars that they had worked on, leaving long black streaks on the asphalt with controlled skids.

Once in his apartment Lester poured himself a glass of Johnny Walker Black, drank it quickly and then had a second to enhance his mood for the evening ahead. Dinner was delivered by Dial-a-Steak. It being an occasion, he ordered the sixteen-ounce filet mignon. When supper was over it was nine-thirty. Lester sat the alarm for two a.m. and then lay back in his favorite lounge chair, to rest and reflect before what he hoped would be a transforming moment.

The most transforming moment in his life had happened the summer he was sixteen. On hot days his group headed up the Connecticut River from Middletown to a private spot with a small, deep pool surrounded by rocks visible just below the surface. Jutting out over the pool was a bluff about sixty feet high. They would swim, and there was much bantering about diving from the top into the pool. It was only cheap talk until one sunlit afternoon about five when Lester suddenly appeared on the bluff. He stood there, toes gripping the very edge, and shouted for attention. Before his buddies could react he jumped into the pool and, seconds later, emerged, pumping his fist in the air. That feeling of exhilaration and terror was what he wanted to recapture as he turned forty.

Lester was on his feet at the first ring of the alarm. He drank a cup of black coffee and ate some toast. Then, he took an amphetamine. Descending to the deserted street he walked to his Crown Vic carrying a small black bag that he put in the trunk. His plan, such as it was, was to drive the highways and byways of New York at high speeds and trust that the fates coupled with the keen instincts of the Crown Vic would somehow transform him.

The night was cool with a wind and a threat of rain, but the breeze blowing through the open windows felt good. To his left Lester could see the Hudson's waters being tossed briskly about. There was a cold-looking half-moon appearing every so often from behind low grayish clouds. He quickly accelerated to eighty, and the few cars on the road this late at night, recognizing the make and startled by its speed, despite the lack of lights and sirens, moved over. This provided only modest satisfaction to Lester. When the highway was clear, he would swerve sharply back and forth, testing his reactions.

Quickly they were passing under the thick, black arc of the George Washington Bridge and leaving the city proper. There would be little potential for life-enhancing thrills in Yonkers. He pulled off the Henry Hudson and waited to see if Crown Vic would sense the proximity of the Bronx, whose crime-ridden streets had been its beat. There was no reaction from Crown Vic.

They found a couple of vacant lots where Lester was able to put the Crown Vic through its paces, practicing more wheeling turns. He felt his old skills coming back and thought that he and Crown Vic made a really good combination.

They drove fast up a couple of Bronx streets that were empty. After a short stop they worked their way onto the Harlem River Drive, then headed south with the calmer flow of the East River on their left, keeping their speed to seventy-five miles an hour as East River Drive merged into FDR. As he approached Exit Two on the FDR, he looked up at the Brooklyn Bridge and felt at the same time a definite pull in that direction from Crown Vic. He squealed into a turn, took the exit, and headed over the Brooklyn Bridge into the borough.

Once over the bridge he stopped and shut off the ignition. Crown Vic seemed to be vibrating with excitement. He decided to head down under the bridge for the view across to lower Manhattan, a clichéd view used by photographers putting together big, ugly coffee table books. As he sat there, a blurry memory of a movie popped into his head. The film involved some kind of violent confrontation under this very bridge. That memory, dim as it was, made him nervous.

It was time to prepare. Lester went to the trunk and took out the small black bag that contained a Whelan hands-free siren with public address system and a Code 3 dash laser M5 flash rotating roof light (primary color blue) purchased on the internet. These were installed in short order. He was as police ready as possible. He knew this was in violation of strict laws but said to himself there's danger ahead; I'm only doing this while I'm in harm's way. At the last minute Lester picked the tire iron out of the trunk and put it next to him on the passenger seat. Then he swallowed another amphetamine.

He got back behind the wheel and steered an increasingly eager Crown Vic on past derelict buildings and down dimly lit streets, the last one full of potholes and leading onto a scruffy parking lot. Lester felt Vic was like a two-ton dog dragging him along.

They bumped along over broken asphalt and weedy patches up to a low wooden barrier topped by a rusty chain-link fence right at the edge of the river with a clear view of lower Manhattan and the giant bridge looming darkly above them. The clouds were thicker and grayer now with the moon making only flickering appearances.

About a hundred yards away four men were standing up close to the barrier, wrapped in blankets and huddled around a rather pathetic little fire. Lester assumed they were homeless, although this seemed a strange place to convene. They didn't seem to be troubled by what they must have thought was a police car approaching.

Lester moved a distance away from the river and turned Crown Vic around so they had a view of the entire desolate lot with the men and the river to his left and turned the engine off. As they waited, the plot of the movie came back to him clearly. Lee Marvin—no, that other one, Bronson—had come to this very place, deliberately seeking trouble, armed to the teeth. A self-elected vigilante, Bronson had wandered around looking lost and vulnerable, inviting attack. Immediately six men with smirks and leers on their weak faces obliged, circling him in anticipation of easy prey, tapping tire irons menacingly on their open palms.

Lester swung his gaze to the right. Right on cue, three burly men carrying tire irons were crossing the lot, heading toward the men. Fate and Crown Vic were handing him his opportunity. Lester's throat went bone dry. He hard-knuckled the steering wheel. Man and car versus three thugs armed with tire irons and God knows what else. What were they after? Did the raggedy bunch of men by the fire have money or drugs, or were the thugs just sadistic predators? With a jolt Lester remembered reading in the Daily News recently about a gang terrorizing the Brooklyn waterfront.

In the movie lamb-Bronson had turned lion-Bronson and blasted the malefactors to kingdom come in short order. Vengeance was Bronson's. Death might be Lester's destiny.

For a moment time stopped and he observed all in a still frame: the homeless frozen, seemingly indifferent to their fate; the smirking thugs poised in mid-stride; himself motionless behind the wheel. The tableau dissolved; the thugs were moving toward their prey. There was no choice. Lester knew he had to drive like he had years ago; he had gone too far to back away. He flicked on the searchlight and shone it straight at the perpetrators, hit the switches that sent the blue light on the roof into furious, insistent circles, and activated a siren sound that split the quiet night air. He hit the accelerator with all his might and as he headed straight for the men, shouted into the PA system, "Police! Freeze, you bastards, freeze!" at the top of his voice. The men stopped and then took off as fast as they could. High with the thrill of the chase, Lester followed hard on their heels and yelled, "Police! I said freeze, you bastards!" The men slowed down but didn't halt, so he turned up the volume and siren even louder and braked to a noisy stop just ten yards away from them.

The men stopped running and turned. A couple of them looking frightened, they dropped their tire irons and raised their hands, but their leader examined Crown Vic more closely.

"Stay right where you are. Don't come any closer. You're all under arrest."

Lester's voice had faltered on this last. He slid Vic in reverse in preparation to back away as he saw how close the thugs were. The leader moved toward them pointing.

"Look at the plate. No police markings. He's no more a fucking cop than I am."

He turned to his associates.

"Come on, let's get this asshole, and then we'll have a little fun with the other scumbags. Look at the little pisspot. You can just barely see him."

The other two retrieved their tire irons and fanned out, ready to encircle the car. They had lethal weapons capable of penetrating Crown Vic's armor. But they didn't appear to have guns. Vic was straining to move as if this were the adventure of its short life. Lester knew he could handle Vic. They were an invincible team.

He raced the engine and backed up swiftly until he was a good distance away from the men who were advancing toward him. Patting the dashboard he said, "Let's go." A deadly dance began. Lester revved the engine and then drove the car full speed toward the men, braking with a squeal when he was only a few feet away and then backing away fast before they had a chance to move in behind him. Lester repeated the process over and over, making the intricate moves seem like child's play. There were long flashes of exhilaration and terror. His intent was to break their spirit and chase them away.

But this was not a jump from the river bluff. His opponents were tenacious. The weaker ones flinched but, after being chastised by the leader, rallied. The leader came close enough to swing at the front of Crown Vic and made a dent in the hood. Lester was angry that they were beating up on Vic. He was getting dizzy from the all the twisting and turning and the sudden stops and starts.

He hoped that the homeless guys had gotten away, but they had moved only a short distance and were apparently transfixed, watching the drama unfold. He yelled over the loudspeaker, "Get the hell out of here," and finally it looked like they were moving.

Focusing once more on the two men Lester thought were the more vulnerable, he roared at them and stopped close as usual, but, rather than backing off as he had been doing, kept stuttering even closer in a series of abrupt starts and stops. The two men finally broke and, yelling, "He's crazy," sprinted toward the exit road.

Now he and the leader confronted each other alone. The man was breathing heavily. He must be six foot six, Lester thought. Even so, Lester, approaching sixteen again in his head, gripped the tire iron on the passenger's seat and thought of stepping out of the car and confronting the man in single combat.

Lester had noticed the guy lumbered around pretty clumsily and took a big windup before delivering a blow. He's vulnerable, thought Lester. I can run rings around him. David and Goliath appearing once again, this time under the Brooklyn Bridge. But as he debated, Crown Vic seemed to crave reverse gear. He wants out of here, Lester thought. As the man advanced, Lester prepared to leave the scene.

As he backed off to have more running room, he heard a siren and saw a whirling blue light, and a police car entered the lot, cutting off the two predators. Two cops got out. One corralled the two men and the other raced toward the back fence that the leader was climbing. It was time for Lester to get away, his work done. His tires squealing, he raced past the police, giving them a "thumbs up" and a jaunty wave that he knew would piss them off. He felt like the ruler of the universe with his faithful sidekick. The cops waved at him to stop but he was already out on the exit road throwing dirt and gravel in all directions.

Lester knew that police would be blocking the bridge, so a return that way was out of the question. He headed off deeper into the borough, making several turns until he found himself on a quiet residential street. He pulled over and parked; took all the police equipment and threw it in the trunk. He realized it would be wiser to leave the stuff in a recycle bin but decided he couldn't bear to part with any of it. It was a souvenir of an adventure that had exceeded anything he could have imagined.

The only casualty was the dent in the hood that Lester vowed he would have beautifully restored at the earliest possible moment. He was sorry he hadn't taken revenge on the thug who had done the damage. But at least he wouldn't be preying on helpless people any longer.

Lester dozed in the car until he felt sufficient time had passed. His plan was to head north and get to the city via the 59th Street Bridge. The street was still quiet early on a Saturday morning. To pass the time he had turned on the radio and listened with half an ear until he heard the reporter say, "Police have launched a massive search for a most unusual driver in a Crown Vic outfitted like a police car. The driver was apparently caught in an altercation with three men who are a part of the vicious Giazzi gang beneath the historic Brooklyn Bridge. As the driver who single-handedly demoralized the gang left the scene, the police were able to make the arrests."

Lester turned the radio volume up. He would have been happy if it had awakened the neighborhood. The reporter went on, "He apparently saved a number of homeless men from certain death. The men who didn't leave because they were riveted by the battle to save them, told police that the driver had executed maneuvers to hold off the gang, worthy of the most expert stuntmen, even though he could barely be seen behind the steering wheel. They're grateful to him for saving their lives. When the police arrived and arrested the gang, the mystery driver took off like the Lone Ranger without identifying himself. There have been some hints that the police may push for prosecution if they catch him for numerous breaches of the law. This reporter wonders if the police might be jealous this elusive man, in his modern version of the Batmobile, captured the gang members and they didn't."

Lester gave a cry of joy and headed out of his parking space, ready to celebrate his notoriety. He couldn't resist the urge to execute a few of his patented moves, honking his horn as he swerved back and forth on the street. As he threw the wheel sharply to the left on his fourth swerve and went well into the opposite lane, a car suddenly pulled out. The two cars collided, merging their hoods. Lester wasn't hurt, but he was angry. Why did this asshole pull out, spoiling his pleasure? Couldn't he admire what Lester was doing? Lester honked and both drivers stepped out of their cars. The other guy was listening to the same program. Lester could hear the announcer winding up the story of the "strange encounter."

"To repeat, perhaps the most incredible part of this improbable story, the homeless who witnessed the scene said that the Crown Vic was executing incredible twists and turns as it jousted with the criminals, like a matador in the bull ring. One of the alleged gang members said the car was driven by a tiny madman."

He was a very large man, the kind that on an earlier occasion might have intimidated Lester, but not this morning. Lester felt even bigger. He was invincible. The man, flushed with anger, took a couple of steps in Lester's direction. Then he stopped, looked Lester up and down and said, laughing, "You're the hot shit little driver, the tiny madman, right? I love it when someone makes the police look silly." Lester nodded modestly in acknowledgment. The man stretched out his hand to shake Lester's. Lester took the meaty hand and shook it vigorously. As they faced each other in a celebratory mood hands firmly clasped, Lester could hear the piercing sound of a siren and see in the distance whirling blue lights coming closer and closer.

PROLOGUE

Ted King walked past the fountain on the Lincoln Center Plaza toward the shining glass façade of the Metropolitan Opera. He loved Italian operas where the tenors sang passionate arias to their ladies fair. On this night, however, the opera was not Italian but German. He was attending a performance of Wagner's *The Flying Dutchman* about the cursed sea captain who can only be redeemed through the unconditional and faithful love of a woman.

Ted had become convinced at age thirty-two that he would never be able to express unreserved love, never be able to pour out his heart like the Italians. He was so anxious, not to say desperate, to make a total and lasting commitment. But relationships that seemed full of promise were undone by endless, self-defeating questioning of the depth of his feeling.

Dr. Gerard Binswanger and Ted had been meeting for some time, working without much success on Ted's complex. Ted was at the Met because of a suggestion, an assignment really, from Dr. Binswanger.

"Go see the Flying Dutchman. You think you're the one who must give perfect love. The Dutchman's problem is the exact opposite of yours. He needs the perfect love of a woman to free him. He meets Senta who is ready willing and able to give him that love."

"Yeah, yeah, I know the opera," he said, "Pretty silly stuff. It's not going to change anything."

"All I'm suggesting is give it a try. You don't have to be the prime giver of love. Maybe this will help you to see that love can come to you if you let it."

Ted entered the splendid main hall of the opera house and folded his lanky frame into a balcony seat. The overture swirled like the angry seas the

Dutchman must sail because of blaspheming God. He can only land once every seven years in search of redemption.

Ted focused hard and made his best efforts to empathize with the Dutchman's problem and Senta's desire to be his savior.

After the curtain fell on Act II, he bought a cognac and walked down to the gallery on the lower level to see portraits of notable Dutchmen of the past.

As he strolled through the hall, Ted became aware of someone staring at him. Out of the corner of his eye, he saw a young woman walking toward him who looked vaguely familiar. He turned to face her. She was short and thin with very pale skin and black, black hair tightly coiled in a bun. Her opera outfit was an odd ankle-length black dress that looked as if it came from somebody's attic, along with high-top black shoes. It's either a joke or she's dressed like Senta, he thought.

"Excuse me, but is your name Ted?"

Ted nodded.

"Ted King?"

"Yes, again." He smiled self-consciously.

"I'm Sarah Goldman. You were a couple of years ahead of me at NYU. We took the same class on early nineteenth-century German opera. Remember that class with Professor Wolfschmerz?"

"Not one of my favorites," Ted said.

He paused.

"With all those people in the class, how in the world did you recognize me?"

Ted was always flattered to be noticed.

"I don't know. I've got a good memory for names and faces. You know how women are. Anyway," she went on, "you slouched around in a sort of distinctive way."

Ted pulled himself up straight.

She paused and said, "Right. You still don't stand up very straight, by the way. Let's see what else I remember."

She paused.

"Ah, yes…if I happened to sit near you in class, I could hear you in-sisting that you only wanted to hear Puccini and Verdi, sounding very opin-ionated. But enough compliments. I don't know, I thought you were sort of cute with your big brown eyes and floppy hair that wouldn't stay put."

She stopped and blushed a little

Ted said, "You don't mince words, do you? He was pleased again that she said he was cute, although he would have preferred something sexier.

"Sorry, I get that way sometimes. I suppose when I'm anxious."

That done, she said, "Anyway, what do you think about the produc-tion? I love this opera. Actually I'm doing Senta with a small local company pretty soon." She made a dismissive gesture. "Just some excerpts really. It's going to be pretty bare bones."

"You're singing Wagner. That's heavy. You don't look big enough.

"Oops," he said after a second, "I'm biting my tongue."

She laughed. "Still a little boorish, aren't you? Hey, don't worry. I'm small but I pack a wallop. Anyway, I can dress for the part, right?"

He nodded. "It's terrific."

"I graduated Juilliard a while back."

The bell rang to signal the start of the next act.

"Could we meet for a coffee afterwards? Talk some more about our beloved Professor Wolfschmerz?" Ted asked.

Sarah smiled. "Why not?"

Not only was absolute and unconditional love necessary for the Dutchman's salvation, but the woman who gives that love had to remain absolutely faith-ful in order to remove the curse forever. In Act III, Senta's longtime boy-friend, Erik, who is sick at heart about the Dutchman, stops her and pleads desperately for her love. She dismisses him abruptly and, Ted thought, quite unpleasantly. The Dutchman sees them arguing, but, mistakenly, thinks it's a lovers' quarrel. Senta has failed the fidelity test. He hastens to his ghostly vessel and sets sail as she tries to convince him unsuccessfully of his tragic mistake. As he sails off, Senta climbs to a nearby cliff and hurls herself into the sea, proclaiming her faithfulness and love as she does so.

Just what I need, thought Ted, a woman who adores me and throws herself off a cliff.

After the opera, Ted and Sarah walked across Broadway and had an espresso. After a verbal nod or two in the direction of Professor Wolfschmerz and some small talk, Ted ordered brandy.

"Tell me about your production."

"Well, it's going to be semi-staged in a little theater deep in the wilds of Tribeca."

She thought for a couple of seconds and went on.

"You know, Senta's kind of strange, really. She's dreamy, kind of remote from reality. She wants to give a passionate and perfect love. But she has to prepare herself in order to move into the Dutchman's realm. That's what I'm trying to do.

She seemed ready to say more but stopped.

"Sorry. I don't want to bore you."

"No. No, I understand," Ted responded quickly. "Love is about transcending yourself somehow." Then he became embarrassed.

"Okay, now we're even. I don't want to bore you either."

Sarah's eyes widened. "Are you kidding? I'm fascinated. You're honest about your vulnerabilities. I like that. More, please, more. I'm all ears."

Ted was still embarrassed, but amazed himself by saying, "Okay, you asked for it. I feel like that kind of love is beyond me. I spend so much time worrying about whether I'm in love or not that I ruin it for the woman and myself."

Sarah looked at him sympathetically

Ted forged ahead.

"I'm seeing a psychiatrist. He sent me here tonight. I have, I blush to use the term, a sort of commitment problem."

Sarah recoiled in mock horror and then laughed. "Who doesn't? So what's the Dutchman got to do with that?"

"Can we talk about later?"

"Yeah, I'd love to hear it anytime. I have a few things going about commitment that I'd like to share. But, maybe tonight is not the night."

"I'm having a good time tonight," Ted said.

She smiled. "Me, too."

She hesitated for a moment, then said, "So, let's get together again, huh? Go to a movie or something? Talk some more about Professor Wolfschmerz? Whatever. You seem to be a nice guy."

"Thanks. I think I am even if I can be a little boorish." He diluted the sarcasm with a wave and said, "Yeah, that'd be fun."

They shook hands and made a date for the following Friday night.

What just happened Ted said to himself on the way home. I never told anyone so much about myself so soon. She might be some sort of kindred spirit. But I'm just here to learn, not to stick my neck out.

They met at 7:30, three nights later, for a light supper and some wine at a small café in Tribeca; the idea was to follow that with a movie. Sarah had shed her forbidding outfit and let her hair down. She was wearing black slacks and a white blouse unbuttoned enough to display a pleasurable expanse of white skin.

"You look great," Ted said.

They had supper and wine and dessert and brandy again; they skipped the movie and talked nonstop until they were alone in the place.

"I didn't open up the other night the way I wanted to, and you did, about love and commitment," Sarah said. "I've been in several relationships and drove myself crazy trying to decide whether I was in love or not, same as you. I can't seem to feel it. I think I'm a pretty nice person and not bad looking and I'm a good singer. And I guess it's okay to say I like sex. So what? When it comes to sticking with a relationship there doesn't seem to be anything there. It makes me sad."

"I'm very sorry. I know how that is," Ted said. "So, Senta?"

"Yes, my Juilliard advisers told me I shouldn't push my voice with Wagner. But I was getting sort of desperate and felt, maybe, if I could get into the part, it might well, ah, transform me."

"Hmm, are we made for each other or not?" offered Ted. "Can two people negative on love make a positive?"

There was an awkward silence that Ted broke.

"I just meant we seem to have a lot in common here. That's all. Dr. Binswanger, my psychiatrist, said I need to get a new perspective. He thought it might be good to see an opera where the man can't do love without some help from a woman."

"Well, I'm glad you guys agree we're worth something even if it's only a rescue mission."

Ted blushed.

"Got you there, huh? Hey, come on, I think your shrink hit the nail on the head. Has it helped? Is Senta getting to you?"

Ted uttered a noncommittal, "Too early to tell."

"Well you're certainly not cursed like the Dutchman. You're trying to fight that nonsense in a shrink's office. I'm trying to break a curse on stage. Art and reality, hand in hand. But don't think I haven't spent some time in a shrink's office too."

She paused.

"Look, let's join forces here," Sarah said. "I've got a rehearsal Tuesday night. What would you think about dropping in?"

"That sounds interesting."

"We're going to focus on Act Three, where the Dutchman screws everything up because he sees Senta and her old boyfriend Erik together and thinks she has been unfaithful."

"Yeah, I remember. He sails away, and she jumps off a cliff to her death."

"Hey, maybe you can help me get into the mood?" Sarah said impulsively. "I do a sort of method thing before the rehearsal. Maybe this will help you somehow, too, although I am not sure how."

Ted found himself becoming more intrigued. She was so direct and honest and she had looked very attractive dressed up. She was much sexier than he had thought when she was outfitted like Senta. He caught himself and stopped, reassuring himself that they were engaged in role-playing and problem solving; nothing that required him to probe his deepest feelings and mess things up again. It was quite refreshing.

The rehearsal building was in an area of particularly decrepit-looking warehouses near the Hudson on the Lower West Side. A heavy mist was drifting in from the river. It was spooky. He creaked his way up to the fifth floor in the freight elevator and stepped out directly into a gloomy, cavernous room. Props were meager. In the center of the room was the spinning wheel, leaning slightly because one leg was shorter than the others. In one corner, there was a high mound that seemed to be made up of a pile of pads covered with tarpaulin that Ted knew was passing for the cliff. The neighborhood and the lugubrious setting struck Ted as being just right for the Dutchman mood and, at the same time, very depressing.

She introduced him to the three men there. The performers were Vladimir, playing the Dutchman, who looked sour and over-bearing and to whom Ted took an instant dislike; and John, the unlucky boyfriend Erik, short and blond, a little unsure of himself. Ted liked his looks: honest and straightforward. The third man, Matthew, the director and rehearsal pianist, was a bouncy, cheery fellow who was doing his best to sound like a Broadway director, full of "darlings" and "sweethearts" and "oh, fucks" when exasperated.

Sarah was back in her Senta outfit that he was taking a dislike to. Vladimir was fully costumed and looked silly in a full black cape and a black musketeer hat with a long white feather sticking out of it. The other two were casually dressed.

"Would you help me get into the mood?" Sarah asked.

"I'll try but isn't it better if you do it; slip into the mood on your own."

"Hey, it's not that easy to get engaged. This set doesn't inspire."

She waved him to a chair and stood in front of him and began to stare at him.

"What are you doing?" Ted asked warily.

"I'm trying to think about the glory and majesty and mystery of a great love unto death."

Ted squirmed in his chair.

"I'm sorry, Sarah, but I don't think this is going to work. It's making me self-conscious."

"Ted, just a little bit longer. I know it seems sort of weird but it helps me."

Ted tried to hold her stare. He felt sympathy for Sarah. He knew how hard she was working to get into the mood. He knew from personal experience the agony of trying to capture a state of mind about love. Along with these charitable thoughts he couldn't help thinking how easy it would be to make jokes about this and felt guilty. But Ted was pretty sure that some of the mental contortions he went through over love were just as silly.

The artists began to rehearse the final act, starting with Erik and Senta's confrontation. As he watched, he felt himself rooting for Erik, who, after pledging his undying love for Senta, was being rejected.

Then it was time to rehearse the last scene where the Dutchman sees them together and misinterprets what Erik and Senta are up to. Senta jumps from the cliff to her death to prove her love. Sarah sang with great passion as the end neared, but for some reason it didn't sound finally convincing to Ted. She headed resolutely up the crude, asymmetric pile that represented the cliff. She kept climbing and, as the music reached its towering climax, she leapt high, off the back and out of sight.

No sound came from behind the cliff. Ted hoped she might have been transformed, as she wanted to be. He couldn't restrain himself and ran around behind the cliff. Sarah was sitting holding her left ankle, sitting under the cliff that was about seven feet off the ground. Matthew arrived right after him.

"Oh, shit, my ankle. I twisted it when I landed."

She started to get up and winced with pain. Ted helped her over to a couch, saying, "Let's get some ice on that."

"What can we do?" Matthew asked.

"Nothing, thanks. She reached for Ted's hand and waved them off.

"Ted's going to stay with me, it's okay. I know you guys need to rush. I'm fine."

Everybody including Ted looked surprised. There was a short silence.

"Sweetie, next time we'll have a bigger, softer mat," said Matthew. "I don't want my Senta coming a cropper."

He looked at Ted, not sure of what was going on.

"You're staying, Ted?"

"Yeah, ah…if she wants me to."

Sarah sat on the edge of the couch, hurt and wired up. After a while, she said, "Thanks for sticking around."

"Why did you want me to stay?"

Sarah shrugged and mumbled something he couldn't understand. He decided not to press the point.

"I wish I could do that last scene again," she said. "I think I was getting the feeling of dedication better."

"Sarah, come on, it sounded fine. Time to stop soul-searching. Take a look at the ankle. Looks like it's swelling up."

Ted found some ice in a small refrigerator and put it on her ankle. He brought her a glass of water and helped her lie back on the couch. Sarah rested for a while. Then, she sat up and beckoned for him to come and sit beside her on the couch. "Can we just sit a minute while I calm down?"

"Sure," said Ted.

After a while, Sarah said in a quiet voice, "I push, push so hard to get the mood right, but it never quite gets there. I wonder all the time how Senta manages to keep inviolate in body and soul when she is preparing for his arrival.

"Maybe you could try not trying so hard?" said Ted. "That's what I'm trying to do."

"Well, bully for you; sterling advice." She looked at him and said, "When you figure out how to do that, let me know."

Ted winced.

"Sorry," said Sarah. "The ankle isn't helping my mood tonight."

"I have a serious question, though, given what just happened. Is it really necessary to have that stupid cliff for these rehearsals? It's danger-ous."

"Absolutely," Sarah answered. "I've insisted on it. I need that sense of danger and possibility, of not knowing what's going to happen when I jump. I'd feel lost without it somehow."

"Well, tonight was a big point for the danger side."

"Okay, next topic," he went on. "I'm very interested in all of this. Is Vlad helping to make this happen? He's the one you're supposed to be swooning over."

"Don't worry. I'm not swooning over him."

"It was a perfectly innocent question."

She frowned.

"Okay, Mr. Innocent, I think he's a pretty good singer but what a pain in the ass."

"So, maybe that colors your interpretation."

"Well, it certainly shouldn't. This is supposed to be art, right?"

Ted couldn't gauge the level of conviction in Sarah's statement. He wondered if might be different if he were the Dutchman, possessed of course with a powerful, trained voice.

Anyway he felt good just sitting with Sarah. He liked talking with her, arguing with her. She looked vulnerable and appealing sitting there. Ted wanted to make sure she was comfortable. He also had a powerful urge to hold her and rub her. He was on the verge of asking her if she was holding herself inviolate like Senta but refrained. She was sitting next to him in pain, and he knew what her answer would be: She had to be like Senta in all re-spects and remain pure for the Dutchman in order to have the breakthrough she wanted so badly. He understood that and, at the same time, was irritated.

Anyway, they were just two people with similar problems. Maybe, at some point she'd make the overture; that was the role she was supposed to play.

Since they were hanging out and talking, there was another point that Ted wanted to make.

"Anyway, I have to say I think the Dutchman is much too hasty in taking off," he said. "And, you know, I think Senta makes a mistake in her choice of men. What about poor Erik? She disses him completely."

"You don't get it, do you, or else are you trying to bug me? This is music and emotion way over Erik's head. The Dutchman is a genuine tragic figure who needs a strong woman to save him. Erik is a pimply teenager. He's the antithesis of tragic. He'll recover. He's not cursed. He's not going to hell or anything like that."

"I don't know," Ted responded. "He hurts as much as anybody else. And he's done nothing to deserve it. He's just in love. That's his only problem."

"Ah, Ted, I think I see what's happening here. Erik has got what you'd like to have, right? His love is unequivocal."

She looked at him hard.

"Look what's happens to him. He loses out."

"Yeah," Ted said, "to that big selfish guy who has so little faith in Senta, he takes off and leaves her flat or so messed up she flattens herself jumping off the cliff."

"Well, Buddy boy, you're sound more pathetic than Erik."

Ted put both hands in front of him, palms up, stopping himself from going further.

"Touché. Okay. Look, I'm sorry. I know how stressful this is. I have to say we both know how to hurt. How about a truce here? Believe me, I'm trying to tell you things that maybe could be helpful, trying to tell them to myself about my own situation, too."

He paused, hoping she was hearing him. "I don't want to argue with a singer who just damn near broke her ankle over a Dutchman and okay, you're right about Erik and me. I admire him, envy him. I wish I were more like him."

He waited.

Sarah said in a controlled voice, "I think we better quit here. Thanks for the ice and the support. Now please go."

Ted said, "Hold on, there. Isn't there something more I can do? I'd be glad to stay. I promise I won't say a word."

"I'm okay. I need to stay alone for a while. The ankle will be all right."

"What about the neighborhood? Don't you want a lift?"

"No, I'm fine. It's easy to get a cab. Anyway, please just go."

"Okay, good luck."

When he arrived on the street it was raining. Ted decided he had better wait and make sure Sarah was really all right.

Sarah emerged after half an hour and walked slowly, with a slight limp, up the street. He followed at a distance and waited until she got into a cab.

They met for supper two nights later and Sarah was still limping. He was going to let her bring up the other night, but her first remark made him wonder if she'd even thought about it.

"I want your honest judgment on this. I want you to tell me whether I'm convincing when I make the final sacrifice," she told him.

"I thought we'd gone beyond this, talking the other night. Anyway, I've already told you I think you're getting it. But I have only heard the finale once. Anyway, what about Matthew and the Dutchman? They are the ones that count."

"Bullshit. You're the judge of all-out declarations of love, right? I want to hear from you."

"I'm the person who can't make any kind of a declaration. I'm here to learn. Are we going to get into another fight?"

Sarah ignored him. She did look desperate.

"Ted," she said, reaching out her hand to him, "I need you to tell me."

"Well, I'm pretty convinced," he began tentatively.

Then, taking a deep breath, he plowed ahead, deciding he had nothing to lose.

"I don't know. I have to say I think you're holding a little something back. Like I said, it could be a little better, that's all you need, a little better. "

Ted looked at Sarah, whose look was now both desperate and perplexed

"This isn't what you want to hear, but if you want to know what I really think, I think you're not really the Senta type. You're a much better person. She's noble and wonderful and sort of full of shit. I think she gets carried away with herself and her mission a bit. You're so much honest than she is. I like you a lot more than I like her."

Sarah started to talk, but Ted raised his hand.

"Let me finish. You're a fine singer. You don't have to be Senta to sing a terrific Senta. Let Sarah do it."

He paused.

"I'll say it again. I like you very much. I think you're great, really. I think I'm channeling my inner Erik and he's starting to wake up and push me."

They sat there, saying nothing. Sarah broke the silence.

"Ted, I don't know what's going on here. I've got to go."

"I'm telling you with less Ted-like reserve that I really like you."

"Okay, okay. I guess that's nice but I don't know what the hell is going on here. You're confusing me. Please don't say anything else."

"I'll see you at Thursday's rehearsal," Ted said.

Sarah shrugged and left. Ted sat a while longer, thinking that he really didn't know what was going on either.

Matthew and Vladimir eyed him suspiciously when he arrived. Sarah had told him that his presence bothered them. They thought that it was distracting her. He nodded to them both and tried to stay discreetly near the elevator. John shook his hand warmly. Ted and Sarah exchanged nods.

Matthew declared, "Sweetie, I've been softening things up behind the cliff. Going to keep working on it. But let's fake the jump, okay? No more bouncing around back there tonight, please."

Before the final scene, Matthew cautioned Sarah once more not to jump. She looked distracted. Ted put himself on alert. As the music reached its climatic point and she started up the cliff, Ted knew she was going to jump. He leapt to his feet and sprinted toward the rear of the cliff. Matthew yelled, "What the fuck's going on?"

Ted arrived behind the cliff just as she jumped. He tried to catch her, but the impact was too great and they crashed together to the floor, Sarah directly on top of him, cushioned from the worst of the blow.

Ted's wind was knocked out. Sarah, at first, wasn't focused on what had happened. When she realized he taken the brunt of her fall, she murmured, "Ted, are you all right?"

Matthew and John came rushing around the corner. Sarah was struggling to her feet.

"Jesus Christ, Sarah," What the hell is going on here?"

"Sorry," said Ted, "but I knew she was going to jump."

Matthew raised his eyebrows over that and then said, "Okay, right. Thanks for protecting her on the way down at least."

She bent over and looked down at Ted. "How was that?" she asked.

"Best yet," Ted managed to gasp. "I think you're getting it if you don't kill us both first."

Matthew became more civil.

"Ted, I don't know what's going on with you two, but, anyway, thanks. Sarah is taking all this too seriously. She needs someone to protect her from herself."

Then back to business.

"Okay, we've got a show to put on. Let's take a break—a good long break—and then try this one more time. I wish we could quit after that episode, but this is the last chance with our distinguished little group here. We've got our full cast rehearsal, such as it is, in three days, and, then, the dress."

Turning to Sarah he said, "That was terrific. But for Christ's sake, Ms. Goldman, please, no jumping. No jumping. No jumping. No jumping. Say it after me. No jumping. Got it? Keep the music; that was great; scrap the jump."

Then, turning to the Dutchman he said, "Vlad, I need a little more passion from you."

Vlad scowled heavily.

"Well, you heard him," Ted said to Sarah as they rested. "You hit it out of the park, you silly shit, even though you almost broke your leg and busted me in two. I heard Sarah that time myself."

She smiled at him.

"Whew, I don't know. I'm getting dangerous in the process. Thanks for having my back or front or whatever it was."

"You felt pretty good even traveling as fast as you were," Ted said.

Sarah gave him a punch.

Ted heard Matthew saying in the background to Vladimir and Eric, "Keep an eye on our jumping jack and her eager friend. The next time could be fatal."

Once again Eric and Senta went through their sad quarrel, and once again the Dutchman and Senta confronted each other. Ted could see that Vlad was miffed at the criticism and working hard to throw more passion into his role. Sarah sounded totally convincing.

The moment came for Sarah to climb the cliff for the ultimate sacrifice. He saw Vladimir and John both bracing themselves. Ted again found himself on his feet and dashing toward the cliff. Yes, of course she was going to jump. He was going to make sure she was able to do that, and he knew he had to jump with her. He brushed John aside. Vlad grappled with him, but Ted shoved him away. He headed to the top, feet squishing in the softness of the ersatz cliff.

Sarah turned in his direction, looking as if she expected him. At her final words, "I'll be true to you until death," she smiled at him. The two clasped hands high above their heads, looked into each other's eyes, and, together, took the leap.

AN URGENT MATTER

The elderly couple boarded the bus just ahead of me, the husband holding his wife's arm. I paid little attention to them except to note that their overcoats were a bit seedy-looking. I passed by them because they were having some difficulty paying their fare and then in turn stood aside as they moved to their seats. The woman looked at me and politely nodded her thanks. They sat close to the driver on the left side. I took a seat several rows back on the other side.

After this short distraction my mind was quickly pulled back to its prevailing obsessive pattern. I had been concerned I'd be late in getting to Albert Hall for a long-anticipated concert, so I left without a last reassuring visit to the loo. As the bus lurched down Finchley Road toward the center of London I was being punished for my laxity. I knew that I would be compromised and not be able think of anything else or enjoy an iota of pleasure until the next opportunity arose for a visit, which would be the men's at Albert Hall, time permitting. My mind was already prodding me to take action; insisting that otherwise I would be intensely uncomfortable, unable to enjoy the concert, and might be endangering my health by engendering a bad case of constipation and a perpetual migraine. But such a mandated visit I knew from bitter experience does only quell momentarily the concern, and shortly my obsessive side would be making even persistent demands. It is never honestly quite clear what the horrific consequences of non-obedience will be. The anxiety mill grinds so fine and intensely and for so long you eventually do what you're urged to, knowing it's wrong, hoping for relief even if temporary.

Trying to change the subject, I would glance periodically at the elderly couple. They chatted in a desultory way for the most part, although the woman at one point reacted strongly to something the man said. After a few quiet words from him, they settled into what seemed to be a comfortable silence. I envied them that close familiarity where only a few words are necessary to convey an understanding or a thought.

"Take at the first sign of irregularity," announced the smug slogan staring down from the large advert board near Lord's Cricket Ground adding an unwelcome exclamation point to my brooding.

As always I tried to fight back. "Bother the first sign of irregularity," said I, in muffled, but firm response to the reminder of the advert board. I tried to think of the visceral discomforts our valiant soldiers must have suffered as thousands of brave Zulu warriors pressed down on the small British force trapped behind their meager fortifications at the Battle of Rorke's Drift, a long ago moment of glory in the Empire's history. But at least the men had ample provocation and proceeded to act so heroically that the Zulus suspended the assault and saluted their bravery. No such salute or recognition of my difficult struggle will ever be forthcoming. That battle goes on in inner darkness.

As an aside (in an attempt to demonstrate my essential normality and give some historical relevance to my military metaphor), I want to reference a marvelous movie called Zulu depicting this battle made in 1964 and starring, among others, Sir Michael Caine in his very first role. I will say I doubt very much that the man Sir Michael was portraying during or after the battle suffered the same fate as I.

How embarrassing for an otherwise mature adult to go through life coiled up figuratively with his large intestine. That's the other demoralizing aspect. Who can I talk to and share this? It is not a subject to discuss with friends. While the pre-adolescent is free to display (nay, insists on displaying) his fascination with the rather limited humorous capabilities of the digestive system and a gang of twelve year olds can spend many a happy hour seeing who can out-flatulence the other, for me this is not part of a rite of social passage nor does it have any aspect of mirth. It's the purest form of mental torture, ludicrous and crazy as it must seem to anyone not lashed to that particular wheel.

What's happened to old Bertram? He's gone a bit crackers; says his mind is betraying him with his bowels. Rather an unseemly affair, that.

Lost in these unpleasant reveries, I was fortunate to notice just in time the bus was at my stop. The couple was descending just ahead of me. Hovering close to them as I waited for their slow descent I was surprised to hear the woman say, "I'm afraid I'll need…before the performance," to which he replied, "Ah, my dear, you've done very well so far but, perhaps, you might have…" and his words trailed off as they walked away. I was quite certain she mentioned the toilet and the husband's rejoinder fit neatly with my own situation. Was it possible that the woman had a similar problem, that a potential ally was sitting near me on the bus?

I could not, in good conscience, follow them closely, so I hurried by and proceeded to the hall. Before going to my seat I intended to visit the exquisite marble restroom facilities. I had been there times before, being an ardent concertgoer, but not since the onset of my obsession six months earlier. Then I was, I believe, a fairly engaging and normal person with a variety of interests ranging from football matches at Wembley to opera at Covent Garden and a good and often engrossing job as a clerk to a barrister at Lincoln Inn with no record of obsessive thinking. Yes, there were times when I returned sheepishly to my flat to make sure the stove was off or the door securely locked, but that didn't take over my life. If security were my current focus I am sure I would lock and unlock, check and recheck the door and finally, hours later, tear myself away only to return terrified that a desperate criminal awaited my arrival, sitting in my favorite chair, knife in hand.

But anyway that is not the obsessive niche I was forced into. I had been feeling lethargic and concluded that a sluggish gastrointestinal tract was the cause. One thought quickly piled on another and then another, soon developing into a scrum of anxiety which identified the colon as the culprit.

Arriving at the entrance to the men's I decided, yet again, to take a stand against my inner Zulu, to see if I could resist the devilish temptation: just do this and peace and enjoyment of the concert will be yours. So I simply stood at the entrance, admiring the splendid marble sinks with silver faucets, the high ceilings with a Grecian frieze around the top, the slabs of marble separating the urinals, and the wooden doors on the stalls with their polished brass handles. Portraits of great leaders hung about on the walls gazing down at man at his most vulnerable would not have been at all out of place. I gazed at this splendor, admired, and resisted.

Pleased with that small success, I reentered the hall.

Just as I took my seat, the elderly couple appeared and took their seats in front of me. The fates were at work. Their plebeian outer garments had concealed terribly handsome evening clothes. They were patrician in profile, clearly people of good birth and breeding, the man, his silver hair brushed neatly back, his thin mustache carefully maintained, the woman, her gray hair carefully bobbed, looking about her with quiet dignity, but my sensitive antennae detected anxiety layered beneath that calm exterior.

I was truly not attempting to eavesdrop, but because the man was speaking in one of those stage whispers that carry, I could not help but hear, "I'm proud of you for not rushing to the toilet, dear. You know Dr. (I didn't catch the name) has told you to try to resist the urge. Distract yourself. Think about your lovely rose garden, that sort of thing. Remember he said you are healthy and very regular indeed, and that this silly business is really a matter of mind over matter."

Despite his words, he looked peeved rather than proud. I saw his wife winced when he spoke of "this silly business," but she smiled wanly and gave a tentative nod. I became excited and felt a complete empathy. Of course her husband didn't understand. If you are not living with it, one cannot possibly know or feel what this silly business is really like. With the proximity of a possible soul mate I felt the full force of my desperation at not being able to share my most embarrassing dilemma with another human being and give and receive compassion.

The concert commenced, and I was quickly at one with the bubbly joy of Mozart's *The Marriage of Figaro*'s overture in the key of D major. When it ended I clapped enthusiastically. Next on the program was Beethoven's Second Symphony in C. While the applause was still continuing, I saw but could not hear a hurried exchange between the man and the woman whose fate I had now linked with mine.

The roiling vivaciousness of the music had provoked a different effect in her. She started to rise. The man tried to stop her, but she brushed his hand away and was off and down the aisle, moving as quickly as she could. My fall from Mozartian heights was instantaneous. Suddenly it was imperative that I rush in order to avert discomfort during the Beethoven. I quickly edged, apologizing, past irked patrons, and headed up the aisle toward the rear of the hall. There was no time to lose.

The lady was just ahead of me, maintaining an erect carriage but, at the same time, trying to move with some speed. At one point she turned to look behind. I hoped she saw me and would recognize me as the polite young man on the bus. She headed left toward the ladies' and I right to the men's. We emerged at the same moment. I nodded for her to go first and bowed slightly. She looked at me and, again, gave a formal nod in return.

Back in my seat, after what proved an unnecessary trip in any practical sense but one that satisfied my insatiable obsession for a short time, I kept looking at the back of her head trying to read her thoughts. As the Beethoven commenced, I became consumed with the idea that I should damn our British sense of reserve and find some tactful way to engage her on the subject that I was now sure was adversely affecting her life as much as it was mine.

The fourth movement of the symphony, unfortunately, had a jumpy, bilious quality to it. (I had read and forgotten that Beethoven himself was having digestive difficulties as he was writing this symphony in addition to his deteriorating hearing.) At intermission she remained in her seat, looking straight ahead.

I hoped that her husband would leave her alone. Wouldn't there be some salvation in an exchange of our deepest concerns, a humanizing sharing similar to that which occurred during the Battle of Britain, when lords and commoners stood shoulder to shoulder in defiance of the tyrant Hitler? But, of course, one doesn't simply tap on a person's shoulder and say, "May I converse with you about the mutual state of our bowels?"

The matter had to be handled delicately. I pondered how I might make an approach that would not cause them to summon an usher or a bobby to eject me. Finally I came up with a tolerable plan. I always carried a couple of sheets of paper in my coat pocket in case I want to jot down a thought or an idea. I would write a note and hope that there would be an opportunity to deliver it.

I spent the remainder of the intermission preparing this message:

"Please forgive my boldness, and if what I say is offensive or incorrect, I ask your forgiveness in that regard as well. I had to speak on a matter I believe to be of the utmost importance to both of us. I was on the bus from Hampstead and seated behind you during this fine concert. From what I have observed and heard (I may be declared guilty of eavesdropping as well) it is my sense that you suffer as I do from an obsessive focus on the workings of the colon. (This is as delicately as I can put it.)

"If there is any merit in my assumption, then I wish you to know that I have full understanding of the unmitigated pain and shame that results from this unfortunate condition. I hope you are able to find an answer in the very near future.

"Once again, I apologize for my intrusiveness, but I felt I could not forgo this opportunity to connect with you as a fellow sufferer.

"From one who understands"

While I wrote I stole occasional glances at the woman and saw her squirming in her seat trying to find a comfortable position. Husband and wife were not speaking. From time to time she would turn and look about the hall. When I saw this I would smile in as noncommittal way as I could, attempting to suggest some acquaintance. With, perhaps, five minutes to go before Brahms Fourth Symphony in E Minor commenced, she rose to her feet, ignoring her husband's restraining hand, and worked her way out to the aisle against the aggravated grain of the returning concert goers. I turned to watch her rush up the aisle with something approaching love in my heart.

The music, full of melancholy, had started before she was back, her face red and her jaw set as she worked her way up the row. Only then could I focus some attention on the Brahms, which I knew well and loved deeply. I have always especially treasured the fourth movement: A simple theme, based on a scale-like eight-note phrase taken from Bach, provides the bare skeleton on which the master erected a monumental structure of thirty variations, each one more heavenly than the last. The same part of me, perhaps, that saw the magnificently appointed men's in a different light in my present situation noted an inverse parallel in the Brahmsian structure. While my own mental theme had started in a simple way, its numberless iterations were not variations but repetitions that only looped around and around on themselves, remaining steadfastly earthbound. The Brahms un-folded living, organic, while my repetitions were inorganic. I was intrigued with this thought, but it was not the time to examine it further and, in any case, its relevance was no doubt limited.

I managed to derive some pleasure from the transcendent finale even as it mocked my own pedestrian thought patterns. The symphony ended and thunderous applause echoed through the hall. The time was drawing near for my attempted spanning of the bridge to this stranger whose plight I knew and shared.

The couple was slow to rise, so I waited, pretending to be absorbed in the program notes. They conversed once more, with the husband having increasing difficulty suppressing his irritation and the wife looking embar-rassed but steadfast. Finally they rose, but rather than following the balance of the audience out the side exits, they headed without speaking toward the back of the hall. I had an urge to rush to her and say, "You don't need to do this. Remember what Dr. 'X' told you. Think of your rose garden."

I simply followed a decent distance behind. As she entered the ladies', I came abreast of the husband and nodded politely. Agitated as he was, he barely nodded back. Then he suddenly turned and entered the men's. No sooner had he disappeared than his wife came out into the hall too quickly, I thought, to have made anything but a token use of the facilities. I looked at her, and when she looked at me I hoped it was with some familiarity. Once more I nodded (this was becoming a bit tedious) trying through my mute look to convey a sense of the connection we had that went beyond ordinary categories.

Then I moved closer and with a bow extended the folded message to her, saying, "I apologize for my forwardness, but I ask you most sincerely to read this. I think we have a malady, a malady of the mind, in common." She looked surprised and started to turn away. Then, not wishing to be rude or for whatever reason, she took the note and placed it in her purse just as her husband reappeared.

They turned and headed down the aisle to leave the hall, not speaking. The woman tried to take the man's arm and he shook her off. She had accepted my offering. I was tempted to follow and see if she might throw the note in a waste can. I had at the last minute added my name and address along with one more sentence: "If I can be of any service to you in this matter or if we might be of mutual service to each other, I would be very pleased." She left the hall carrying that white sliver of hope with her.

As I stood watching the door where they exited, my mind shrilled a reminder of the lengthy trip back to Hampstead and what agonies might ensue if I missed my last chance just a couple of meters behind me. I turned and entered the men's room, now dimly lit and empty. Shadows flattened the grandeur that had inspired my resistance earlier in the evening.

WIN'S WAR

Win's two heroes were his father, Robert Winter Billings, and Bobby Wilson, the Redbirds' slugger, better known as the "Bomber."

His father, a foot surgeon, was short and quick. Win particularly liked his hands, which were small-boned with long tapering fingers. Bobby Wilson pushed up to six feet four inches tall and out to two hundred sixty pounds. Win had an old photo cut out of a Gazette sports section, which showed only the Bomber's big hands, his thick fingers with lots of dark hairs. Win hoped his hands would never look like that. But he wanted the power Bomber had, the strength to pound the ball out of the park in the bottom of the ninth, trailing by two with two men on and two outs. Could anything be more wonderful? he thought.

Win felt guilty sometimes because he admired the Bomber so much and was afraid of hurting his father's feelings. He tried to balance things out in his head as best he could. When I grow up I'll probably want to be a doctor like Dad, but maybe I could be in the majors for a little while before I go to medical school.

On September 7, 1951, Win heard the terrible news on the radio that the Bomber had to go into the Army Air Force the day after the season ended. He'd be flying real bombers in Korea before very long.

The next night Win dreamed that his father and Bobby Wilson (that's what his father always called him) were talking together on a street corner. At first, they seemed to be very friendly. Win was there in the dream, too, watching them from a few yards away. Pretty soon, though, they began to argue and point at Win, who couldn't hear what they were saying. He wanted to get closer and tell them to be friends, but his feet were stuck to the ground. His father put out his hand, trying to patch things up, the way he always did. The Bomber took his hand but, instead of shaking it, started squeezing as hard as he could. His father got a twisted look on his face, but he didn't cry out. Wow, poor Dad, Win thought, the Bomber is so strong. I've got to do something. Just then, Win's feet came unstuck. He headed toward them with no idea what he would do, yelling, "Stop! Stop!"

Suddenly the Bomber started getting dimmer and dimmer, wasting away like the Wicked Witch of the West at the end of *The Wizard of Oz*, except Bomber didn't end up in a puddle. He just vanished. Win knew the Bomber still had a grip on his father's hand because it was all bent out of shape. Finally, his father punched hard with his other hand into the space where the Bomber's jaw had been. At last, his squeezed hand dropped to his side. His father still looked to Win like he hurt a lot, but he rubbed his hands together a couple of times and waved at Win to show he was okay. Just before Win woke up, he was worried that his father wouldn't be able to operate any longer.

The news of the Bomber's departure followed right away by the bad dream upset Win. Usually when he was worried about something, he could talk to his father about it. This time he couldn't think of a way to bring it up. The dream seemed to be telling him he couldn't stay loyal much longer to both of his heroes since they were fighting like bitter enemies in the dream. Worse than that, he remembered the part of the dream where they were arguing and pointing at him. Were they fighting over him?

Win and his father already had tickets to the last game of the season, the Bomber's farewell. Win had a brand new baseball that he hoped he could get the Bomber to autograph. His father said they would go to the player's entrance at the end of the game and get the Bomber's signature.

On Sunday, September 26, the last day of the season, they left early for the park. Win sat next to his father, barely able to sit still. There was even more excitement now because the Bomber was just two home runs shy of tying the record of forty-seven home runs hit by Goose Hornly way back in 1931.

"I wonder if the Bomber can do it. The Barons are good and Mike Brown on the mound. Bomber really hates him. Big Mike is twenty and eight on the year."

His father said, "Pretty exciting, huh? It would be great if Bobby Wilson could break the record."

"Dad," Win said after a pause, "Why do you always call Bomber Bobby Wilson?"

"That's his name, isn't it?" his father answered quickly. Then, he said, "I can do better than that. I think he is a great ball player and, how can I say it, maybe not such a good guy. I guess he's just not my idea of a hero, so I don't want to use his 'hero' name. Does that make any sense?"

"Not much."

"Well, let's just go and enjoy his last game. I know you think he's the best. What do you think about Bobby going off to war?

"Why can't they get some other people to fight? He's about thirty. Getting kind of old." Win couldn't stop. "I feel so bad he's leaving."

His father laughed. "Don't tell anybody my secret, kid, but I'm about ten years older than Bobby. I guess we all look ancient to a twelve-year-old."

"Dad, you're a doctor so you can work forever. Bomber hasn't got much time left. What about that jerk, Flanagan, saying in the Gazette that Bomber's not patriotic and tried to get out of going? I don't believe it, but if he did try, so what? There's a million people who can fight, but there's only one Bomber!"

"Easy there, Win! Sorry I brought it up. Let's talk about fighting the war later."

They drove along in silence for a while. His father said, "How would you feel if I had to go off to Korea?"

Win said quickly, "I couldn't handle it!" He paused and then more slowly said, "I'd hate it. But you're pretty old, right?"

His father nodded. "Yeah, I'm pretty old."

Inside the stadium, batting practice was still going on. On their way to their seats in right field, where the Bomber's home runs usually landed, they bought two hot dogs and a program. Win had his well-worn Spalding glove with him in case a ball came his way. The day was clear with rain predicted later in the day. A strong wind was blowing in from right field, off the lake. "Bobby Wilson's got a tough wind today," his father said.

When the Bomber came to bat in the bottom of the first, he hugged the plate and sent a stream of tobacco juice in the direction of the mound. His big hands were wrapped around a thirty-eight-inch Louisville Slugger, daring Mike Brown who dared him right back. Bomber caught the second pitch, an inside fastball, and slammed Number 46 into the right field stands a couple of rows away from their seats. In the fifth inning, Bomber smashed a hanging curve on a line, hit the ball so hard it was still going up when it reached the stands. This time, it hit about four rows away. Number 47. The record was tied! Other than the Bomber's home runs, the Redbirds weren't doing much. The Barons picked up a couple of runs in the bottom of the sixth, so the score was all even.

Next time up Bomber hit two long beauties good for four bases, except they curved just outside the foul pole. "This is it, Bomber!" Win shouted. The next pitch was a fastball way inside. The Bomber tried to back off, but the ball hit him on the right hand. He threw the bat down and started to head toward Mike Brown, who turned away, shrugging his shoulders. Win took that to mean it was an accident. The Bomber shrugged, too, shook his hand a few times and trotted down to first, waving off the trainer. He's not about to get in a fight and lose his chance at the record, Win thought.

A chill developed as the game moved quickly into final innings. The wind was even stronger, blowing big dark clouds full of rain across the field toward home plate. In the bottom of the eighth, the Redbirds got a couple of men on base after the first two batters were retired. The Bomber's final at bat, maybe ever, started after a long, standing ovation from the huge crowd. He took the first two pitches for balls, both inside and close. Mike Brown was giving no quarter.

"Good eye," yelled Win. "Smash it Bomber!"

The third pitch was right where the Bomber liked it. The ball shot off the sweet spot of his bat and set out for the right field seats, turning and pushing against the strong wind. Win thought it looked like it was headed straight for him and felt that a part of his life was up there, tumbling through the air alongside the ball. He stood and stretched out his glove, ready to catch the record-breaking blast.

The ball battled the wind and finally started coming down. Win wanted to close his eyes but couldn't. Pete LoPresti, the Barons' right fielder, was at the base of the fence. As the ball headed into the bullpen, Pete reached high into the darkening sky with his gloved hand and made a great jump, far above the bullpen wall. Pete came down from his flight, clutching the ball in his glove, which he waved triumphantly in all directions. The crowd had been holding its breath but now gave a mighty groan followed by a long silence. Win sat down in a daze. His father let him sit for a while, then, put his arm around him. Soon rain began to fall and the game ended. Win didn't even know who won.

After a while, he asked, "Dad, do you think that Bomber's hand getting hit messed up his swing?"

"No, I don't think so. There's an awful lot of wind. Anyway, he came so close. Listen, what about the autograph? Shall we go get it?"

"Gee, I don't know, Dad. It's raining and I'm cold." He felt awful and wanted to go home. He didn't care anymore about the autograph.

"Win, I really want you to have it. Bobby Wilson almost did it. I think you'll kick yourself if we don't give it a try."

Win knew his father thought he wanted the autograph badly and didn't feel like talking anymore about it. "Yeah, Dad, I guess you're right. Let's go."

At first, there was a big crowd waiting at the player's entrance. Players came out and left but no Bomber. The rain came down harder.

Win said, "What do you think, Dad? He's waiting for everyone to go away so he won't have to sign. That's what they say he does."

"Let's wait a while longer," his father said. "We're soaked anyway."

Soon, they were the only ones left. Finally, the door opened and out came the Bomber. A tall blond woman clung to his arm. She's beautiful, Win thought. Bomber was laughing and lurching a little. He had a beer in his hand and didn't look to Win like he was hurting too much. When his father poked him, Win held out his hand with the sodden baseball. The Bomber started to walk by them without a glance.

He was just about all the way by when Win's father said, "Bomber, we have been waiting for a long time."

The Bomber stopped. He looked hard at Win's father. His father was staring right back at him. This time Win's feet weren't stuck to the ground. He was ready for trouble. He started to move between them.

The woman let go of Bomber's arm and pushed him forward, saying, "For Christ's sake, do it Bobby. They look like drowned rats."

The Bomber came over, signed the baseball and handed it to Win, saying, "Good luck, kid." He nodded to Win's father, then stuck out his hand and said, "You, too, pal."

Win got scared again and yelled, "Hey!"

They both looked at him, surprised, the Bomber with his hand stuck out. His father just took the Bomber's hand, shook it and said, "Good luck in the Air Force." That was that. Bomber walked off in the pouring rain with the woman back on his arm.

"What was that 'hey' about?" his father asked. "You look worried, like we were going to fight or something."

"I don't know," Win said. "Let's go."

Before going to bed, Win put the ball on the table under the giant color photo of the Bomber swinging his mighty swing. As he started to doze off, he thought, again, about the Bomber and his father shaking hands in the dream and then in real life.

The next night after supper, while Win was doing his homework, his father came into the room and sat down on the bed. He said, "Win, I've got something tough to tell you. I got a notice the other day that I am being drafted." He paused. "Like Bobby Wilson. I know that the Army needs doctors badly, but I might be able to get out of it because I have a family. I've pretty much decided not to do that because I don't think it's right. I didn't want to mention it to you until I was clearer about what to do."

Win felt as if someone had punched him right in the stomach. First the Bomber, now his Dad. His father reached over to hug him and said, "I'm going to miss you so much." Win didn't feel like hugging and couldn't think of anything to say. His father went on, "The funny thing is, during the last war, I tried to volunteer, but I had flat feet, so they wouldn't take me. Now I'm going in because I'm a foot doctor."

Win was starting to cry and waved his father away. His father said okay and left the room. Win didn't come out of his room that evening. When he got into bed, he couldn't go to sleep for a long time. I've been talking so much about the Bomber. Now, bingo, Dad's going to war, too. What if he gets shot? Doctors don't get to fight. Except I've seen those pictures of medics right in the front lines with the soldiers lying on the ground. And on and on like that until he finally fell asleep.

He woke up suddenly, turned on the light, and looked at the clock. It was only 2:15. He could hear the rain still pouring down. Win saw the ball sitting in front of the big color picture of the Bomber with his big hands squeezing the life out of the bat. All of a sudden he wanted the Bomber out of his life. He got out of bed, picked up the ball, and went downstairs as quietly as he could and out the back door. He stood in the rain, holding up the ball and then rubbing it until he figured the last of the Bomber's scrawly autograph was gone. Then he wound up and threw the ball into the dark as hard and as far as he could. He hoped it would be lost in the woods behind the house and rot away until there was nothing left. When Win got back to his room, he pulled off his wet pajamas. He grabbed the Bomber's picture off the wall, ripped it into little pieces, threw the pieces into the wastebasket, and got into bed, crying as he did.

When his father got home next evening, Win came downstairs holding two pairs of boxing gloves and handed the larger pair to his father. The gloves were a Christmas present from three years ago. They hadn't boxed in a long time. His father nodded. Without a word, they went down to the small basement room which was their ring.

The minute his gloves were on, Win rushed at this father swinging as hard as he could. He yelled, "Fight! Fight! Man to man! I'm not a baby!" His father fended off a few blows, tried to jab at Win, holding back. Win kept coming on, punching as hard as he could.

As his father dropped his guard and tried to grab Win's arms, one of the wild swings caught him hard in the pit of the stomach.

His father gasped, "Hold it! Hold it! Stop!" He finally managed to get his arms around Win, who was quivering.

Win yelled, "Ouch," loudly and shook his hand a couple of times. The punch had stung. He pulled himself together saying, "I'm all right."

His father said, "Wait a minute. I'm the guy that got slugged." Then he hugged him, and this time Win hugged him back.

"Come on, Win. It's okay." Now his father laughed.

Win said, "Yeah, Dad, I think I'm starting to get over being mad. I've got to grow up sometime." He thought a second. "Funny now everybody's hand has been banged up at least once."

"What do you mean?" his father said.

"Nothing," said Win. "Dad, can we just sit on the floor a minute?"

"Yeah, it's been a tough day," his father said. They slumped down on the floor, side by side.

Back in his room, Win decided the only thing to do was to go straight to bed. He took off his clothes and reached for his pajamas. Then, he stopped and looked at himself in the mirror. His body didn't look any different. I'm different though, he thought. He hoped his body would start to grow up pretty soon and catch up with the other changes in his life, like being the man of the house after his father left for war. Then, he put on his pajamas and got into bed.

LIBERATING WOMAN

Ruth Franklin stood in her garage entrance, ready for her mission: a walk that she hoped would begin a bridge between the white and Mexican communities. She checked one more time to make sure Ellen, just fourteen months old the day before, was secure in the carriage, then released the brake and headed down the driveway. It was shortly after noon on November 1, the Day of the Dead, in Sierra Vista, Arizona.

On the Day of the Dead, the Mexican families arrive at cemeteries early, spend the morning sweeping and cleaning the graves, then decorate them with flowers. They perform acts of respect for their dead. After that, they party well into the night. Ruth thought this custom, shared by many Catholic cultures, was a civilized honoring of departed souls.

A few months ago the Arizona legislature had passed strict immigration laws that had infuriated many and pleased an equal number. Police now had the obligation to check persons if they had reason to believe they might be in the United States illegally. There had been no major disruptions or protests yet. But there was considerable fear in Ruth's neighborhood that it was only a matter of time. Day of the Dead could be the trigger for violence. These fears were stoked by a recent op-ed column in the conservative *Vista* that rumored this and rumored that, and ended with this sentence: "Trouble, like a long black plume of smoke from a smoldering fire, seems to hang over our once peaceable town, thickening with each passing day." Ruth thought the community was alarmist and the *Vista* article provocative.

She wrote a letter of strong disagreement to the Vista that they published, surprised by the intensity of her feelings about the divisions in her town and her willingness to go public with them. What had come over her? Maybe it was something about feeling like an underdog and seeing others in that light.

Honestly she thought it was getting to know her Mexican cleaning lady who came twice a week. Her name was Elena. She had started cleaning three months before. Her story of five children, one of them seriously compromised with a bone disease, an erratic husband, no money and on and on, was not new to Ruth. There were plenty of these horror stories available on television. But this was personal and coming from a woman sitting across from her at her kitchen table drinking coffee. Ruth was amazed at how Elena kept going. She found herself telling Elena about the difficulties in her marriage that had been growing over the last year.

She hadn't consulted with her husband, Sam, about the letter. He was really angry when he read it and yelled at her.

"That was the goddamn stupidest thing you've done yet, and you've done a lot of stupid things. You're making us look like fools. What are people going to say? You know how they feel about the Mexicans being here."

Ruth was a little intimidated. He loomed over her angrily, and she thought he might hit her. But she had let herself be intimidated too long and fought back.

"Yeah? I know how they feel. I think they're wrong. I've been waking myself up to a few things."

"Forget that liberal crap. Go back to sleep again. This isn't New York, and if I have anything to say about it, it'll never be."

"You're the one who's asleep. The world is changing, and you and a lot of our friends are running in place. Everybody's entitled to respect."

"I want you to write a letter to the *Vista* saying it was just a joke. Call everybody we know and tell them you were having a woman's problem and didn't know what you were thinking."

"No. And don't tell me what to do. I'm sick of that. I'm entitled to some respect."

"Okay, great. Hit the streets tomorrow and see how much respect you get. In the meantime get your ass moving and call people and tell them you were crazy. Whatever. Think about me. People will say I can't control my own wife."

"You can handle it anyway you want. I'm not doing anything."

Ruth wished she felt as strong as she thought she sounded.

Many people were keeping their children home from school and were staying home themselves. In the morning, they didn't say a word over breakfast. Sam, macho as always, tried to act nonchalant, but she saw him tuck his revolver into his pocket as he was leaving. He assumed she would be at home all day, making those phone calls. Home was a woman's place, anyway, as far as Sam was concerned, whether it was the Day of the Dead or not.

Ruth had already decided before the fight with Sam. The fight confirmed her in her decision. He'd said, "Hit the streets." That's exactly what she was going to do. She was not prepared to spend the day, clutching her child fearfully and peering through drawn curtains, waiting for trouble. It was time for her to take some action.

Her plan was simply to walk, as a liberated woman, in the year 2011, to the very heart of the Mexican district wheeling her child. She would be respectful and expected respect in return. She might not be welcomed with open arms, but it could be a start to new harmonies and understanding between the two populations.

On her trips through the district, she noticed a store called "Manny's." Manny's would be her destination. She would purchase some of the delicious Sugar Skull Candies, a treat specially made for the Day of the Dead.

Manny's was a considerable distance, but Ruth planned to walk the whole way with Ellen. She walked the length of Birnam Street and turned on Saguaro Avenue. The weather was hot, and she was sweating and uncomfortable in her jacket. Ruth took off the jacket and tucked it away in the carriage. The light shirt under the jacket was already a little wet with sweat. She wondered if her nipples were showing and hunched over a bit at the thought. She didn't want anybody thinking she was provocative.

As the distance from home lengthened, Ruth started to walk faster. She was excited about her project. Ellen started to sing something and Ruth joined in, trying to turn her daughter's tuneless vocalization into a version of "Onward Christian Soldiers" that ended feeling a little too strident. After that, she gave Ellen a cookie.

Ruth was not naïve. She knew that many people would think taking Ellen along was reckless. Her rationale was that Mexican mothers would be wheeling the babies about so why shouldn't she? Mothers with children were safe and respected everywhere. She would be safer with Ellen than on her own.

Ruth was carrying a small revolver. She, and a very large number of other women in town, carried one as a matter of course. Sierra Vista was an "open carry" town, and weapons were seen everywhere. Ruth generally kept hers concealed.

She took pleasure in going to a range. Ruth was a skillful shot; she was actually better than most men, including her husband, Sam, although he would never admit it or give her credit. Carrying a weapon was as natural for her as carrying a pocket book. She put it there without a second thought.

Now Ruth and Ellen were zeroing in on their goal. They turned off Saguaro onto Mexicali Avenue, a melancholy thoroughfare that stretched, dusty and endless, to the intersection with Santa Anna Avenue that was at the heart of the district. Within a couple of hundred yards, the neighborhood changed. The houses were smaller, many needing paint. There was little sign of life. Ruth tried to suppress the feeling that she was being watched. In spite of a resolve not to check, she caught herself a couple of times looking back to make sure no one was trailing her.

She was glad to pass an elderly Mexican couple, sitting on a bench. The man tipped his cap and nodded to her. The woman smiled at the carriage where Ellen was singing away. Ruth smiled and offered a polite, "Buenos días," and bowed in their direction. The couple was her parents' age.

Up ahead on the right was an alley from which a young couple was emerging, wheeling a carriage with two children in it. They headed up the street after glancing in her direction.

Ruth and Ellen were now approaching the intersection of Mexicali and Santa Anna. Near the center of a block of nondescript buildings girded with crumbling stucco was the sign for Manny's.

Ruth slowed her pace and took the precaution of assessing the scene. There were three middle-aged men dressed in loose-fitting white shirts and trousers, lounging and smoking in front of the building one door beyond the store.

She could see the men were sizing her up as a woman and finding her attractive. She was used to that, but they did not appear hostile and she didn't feel threatened. Two of the men were slight and dark-haired, wearing baseball caps. The third was a distinguished looking man, more elderly that the others, with silver hair. He had a very large belly and wore a sombrero. Ruth nodded at them and offered, "Buenos días a todos," and received a nod and a grunt in return. The young couple had preceded Ruth into the store.

She was sure Ellen would love a sugar skull candy. She would have a bite too. This was working out well. "Mommy wants you to stay quiet for the next few minutes , okay?"

She headed into the store pushing the carriage ahead of her. It was dark inside and smelled of strange spices, dirt, and other odors that Ruth couldn't identify and was not sure she wanted to. It took her a minute to adjust to the darkness. The windows in front were dirty, but some sunlight did penetrate the dust-filled interior. Merchandise was stacked in piles, helter-skelter on the shelves. The sunlight didn't penetrate to the back of the store where there were only a couple of bulbs to light that area. The only people in the store were the couple with the children and a woman about sixty who was sitting behind a table on which sat an old cash register. The three were having a lively conversation when she entered, which abruptly terminated. Ruth nodded and said, "Buenos Días," and received a mumbled, "Buenos," and a suspicious look in return. Ruth saw the assortment of sugar skull candies on a shelf but that there were only six left. She pointed and said, "I'll take two please." But just as she spoke, she could see the young woman had her eyes on the shelf as well. Ruth gestured at the candies and asked, "Is this all?"

The cashier burst into a torrent of Spanish that Ruth couldn't understand. Ruth felt she had to follow through.

"How many do you need?" she said to the woman slowly and distinctly.

"Price very good. Big family. All love...."

"Are you saying you want them all?" Ruth asked.

"Please, madam. My children, my family. Is Día de los Muertos."

Her children began to cry loudly, and Ellen, who had been obediently still, joined in.

"Ellen, not now, please, honey."

Ruth looked at the woman who was crying.

What am I doing? Ruth thought. I'm being a bitch.

"Ma'am, you take them all."

Ruth quickly left the store.

The three men had not moved. Ruth was sure that they had heard the commotion, but they showed no concern. She paused and decided she wanted to go back and apologize. She hadn't come all this way to contest with a poor mother who was trying to buy treats for her family.

She left the carriage on the sidewalk and turned to go back into the store just for a second, forgetting to put the brake on. The sidewalk was dramatically tilted away from the store. The carriage with Ellen in it began rolling toward the street. A battered old Ford had been cruising slowly up the street and was directly heading toward the carriage, its driver seemingly oblivious to the danger. Ruth screamed and began to move, but too late.

The older silver-haired man was surprisingly agile. Just as the car was about to hit the carriage, he grabbed the handle bar and twisted it out of the way. The carriage spun around and tipped Ellen out. The man who had made the life-saving lunge fell heavily on his side. The car slowed a little and then moved on.

"Ellen! Ellen!" cried Ruth, picking up her frightened child and hugging her. She screamed for five minutes. When she calmed down Ruth hugged her some more.

"Are you all right? Are you okay?"

She righted the carriage and tucked Ellen in as tightly as she could.

"Oh baby, I'm so sorry. I'm so sorry. Mummy made a terrible mistake."

The men had pulled their heavy friend to his feet. Wincing with pain, he was slumped down on the bench by the door, holding his side.

Ruth went over to the man who had saved her daughter and said, "Thank you so much for what you did. I did such a stupid thing. I hope you're all right."

She put out her hand, but the man just stared at her.

"Can I do anything for you?"

That sounded pretty pathetic. What could she possibly do? She thought for a second about offering him some money but that would clearly be insulting. She felt so guilty that she had put her daughter in harm's way and caused the old man to hurt himself.

She turned and began to push the carriage away. After she had gone a few steps she heard him say, "You should not come here again, lady. Please. You only make trouble. We don't make trouble."

Ruth reddened and said nothing. She pushed them up Mexicali Road toward home, her head filled with images of the carriage rolling toward the street. Ellen was quiet and appeared okay, but what kind of a mother was she? She had let herself be distracted. This was not so far at all the noble mission she had set out on. She had almost gotten her daughter killed. What was that crazy guy in the car doing? What about the poor guy that saved her? I hope he's all right.

Ruth wanted to get as far away from Manny's as fast as possible. She was confused and tired and just wanted to get home. She tried to push the carriage on a run but could only hold that pace for a short distance.

After they had gone a good ways back up Mexicali, Ruth noticed a group of young men some distance away coming toward her. They were spread out across the sidewalk. Ruth became very tense. Would they let her pass? She knew she should go out in the street and pass quietly. She pushed the carriage off the sidewalk. Then she stopped. Wasn't this trip supposed to be about respect and the right to walk the streets freely? She needed to do something to salvage the mess she had created.

Straightening up, she pushed the carriage back on the sidewalk. As the group came closer, she could see that four of them were young, ten to twelve years old, and small. The fifth was about sixteen and tall, with an attempt at a mustache. They stopped about ten yards away and stared at her. Nervous but resolved, Ruth walked closer saying, "I beg your pardon." The four younger ones stepped aside but the oldest did not move. She came to a halt in front of him and said, "Please excuse me so my child and I can go through. This is a public sidewalk." The young man didn't move. The two stared at each other for several seconds. Then, he stepped aside, but as Ruth passed, she was quite sure, even though the impact was very slight, that he had jostled her.

Ruth moved a few paces beyond the group, stopped and turned. Common sense once more told her to move on, but how could she tolerate that kind of behavior? The smaller boys were still giggling and saying what she was sure were admiring things to their leader.

They were getting ready to move on. Ruth couldn't stop herself. Pushing the carriage behind her, she pulled out her revolver and took a firm stance, facing the group. The smaller boys shrank away but the youth stood his ground.

"Young man, you owe me an apology."

"Lady, you wouldn't dare," he said in unaccented English, moving a step toward her.

"Don't push me," Ruth said. "I have every right to be on this sidewalk and expect courteous treatment. I asked you to excuse me. You pushed me."

"Fuck you and your mother, bitch. I didn't lay a finger on your old tired body. Fuck you and the little shit with you."

He waved his arms all around in mock fear. "Oh, she scares me."

Ruth deliberately leveled the revolver so it was pointed at the boy. Then she raised it so the aim was well above his head and released the safety. The boy blanched but held his ground.

"Hey, I said, 'Fuck you and your mother, bitch.' Actually, you're pretty sexy. I'd like to fuck you hard."

Ruth didn't really want to shoot, but she had been grievously insulted. Both held their ground. Ruth's hand on the trigger was shaking; out of control and not intending to do so she pulled the trigger. There was a loud bang. The young boys ran. The youth still refused to move. Ruth lowered the weapon and put on the safety. They exchanged another long, hostile stare. Finally, the youth shrugged and said, "Crazy bitch, you're in trouble now," and walked away.

In a daze, Ruth headed for home at a run, the carriage bumping up and down and Ellen crying loudly. Ruth kept saying, "Oh my God! Oh my God, I've done it again," and, "Please baby, I can't stop right now," and kept on pushing the carriage as fast as she could.

Finally, after what seemed like an eternity, she realized they were back on Birnam Street. It was dusk and very quiet. They were right by a small, well-lit park that she and Ellen often came to. Exhausted, she wheeled the carriage to the nearest bench, put her jacket on, and sat down. Ellen was quiet. Ruth took deep breaths to quiet her own pounding heart. What a disaster her walk for respect had become in her two encounters. She still thought it was a worthwhile thing to try, but whatever possessed her to bring her child with her and to fire the revolver. I couldn't help it. Sam would be seething with anger if he knew. He might want to file for divorce and take custody of Ellen. He'd tell the court his mother could take of Ellen. I'd fight that with my last breath. What a bitch she is. Anyway, I am really a good mother even though I've done something that a lot of people wouldn't understand.

After they had been sitting for about ten minutes, while her mind continued its racing, a police car went slowly past the park, shining its spotlight around. When it settled on Ruth and Ellen, the car stopped. A young officer got out and came over. Ruth did her best to look at ease.

"Lady, are you all right? You shouldn't be here. You should be at home. Especially with that kid."

He looked at Ruth somewhat suspiciously.

"We had a report of a gunshot not too far away a few minutes ago. Did you hear anything? Do you know anything about that?"

Ruth shook her head.

"Maybe it was from the cemetery," she answered. "I hear they shoot off guns over there."

He ignored her comment. "I talked to a bunch of young kids back up on Mexicali Road. They said they didn't know anything about it. They didn't have weapons on them. I'm going to talk to them again. A couple of the younger ones looked as if they were frightened about something. They're not telling the real story."

He turned his attention back to Ruth.

"What are you doing out here anyway? Does your husband know you're here? Don't you know this is the Day of the Dead? You're not really safe here."

"I feel perfectly safe," said Ruth. "I just had to get out of the house for a while. I don't know why everybody is so worried about the Day of the Dead."

The officer said nothing and Ruth kept on talking.

"We needed some air. And as far as my husband is concerned I make my own decisions."

While she was talking she was trying desperately to figure out what to do. She prided herself on being an honest, law-abiding citizen with nothing to hide, but it was better not to get into the whole story. She had enough to deal with already.

She got up to leave.

"I'm on my way home now. I live just up here on Palm Street."

He shrugged. "Do you want a lift?"

"Thanks, officer. I'm fine. I'm going straight home." She added, with the most radiant smile she could manage, "I promise."

The officer shrugged again. "Okay, lady, please do. If you see anything suspicious, please let us know. I'm Officer Swenson. This is my territory tonight. They want me to find out who fired that shot. I am going to talk to those kids again. Something's not right with their story."

The officer was young and earnest, intent on doing his duty.

"Yeah," he added, "and I had to help take some old guy to the hospital from Manny's."

He turned and headed back to the police car.

Ruth had the image of the silver-haired man pulling Ellen out of danger and falling heavily to the sidewalk.

"We don't make trouble. You make trouble," the man had said.

Officer Swenson was approaching the police car. Ruth knew what she had to do. She hoped she could do this without implicating anybody. She called out, "Officer Swenson, come back. I can tell you about the gunshot. It went off with no one around. It was a silly accident."

Swenson turned and headed back in her direction, digging in his pocket for a notebook.

IN THE TRENCHES

The four boys finally found time to go to war once fifth grade ended at noon on Wednesday, June 10, 1942. Right after Pearl Harbor, they had been both thrilled and scared. What if a German submarine lurking in the cold waters of Boston Harbor surfaced on a December night to launch shells at them? But, by mid-January, no missiles had whizzed overhead and crashed into City Hall or any other building critical to Newton's defense. Besides, there were the distractions of school, Cub Scouts, and skating and the humiliations of choir practice and dancing school to keep them occupied. Now, except for choir, all that was over. Besides, Bobby Swift's brother, Pat, a hero to them all, had enlisted in the Marines. They expected him to be fighting the Nazis before long. This gave them a personal stake in the war.

Early in the morning of Friday, June 12, Bobby, Baird Jewell, Dan Munroe, and Johnny Fayerweather reported for duty behind the Munroes' barn. Here's how the new recruits shaped up. Baird was the tallest by a couple of inches and the oldest by about four months and had braces on his teeth. He had been sick a lot during the winter and was still pretty skinny as a result but would be combat-ready soon. Bobby was next in height and age and the strongest, at the moment, with a body that would, in time, become heavy-set like his father, Patrick. His stockiness was offset by a rather fine-boned face and dark, sensitive eyes, like his mother. Baird's father, the Reverend Robert Jewell, was the rector of St. Christopher's Episcopal Church. The Jewells and the Swifts had come to Newton at the same time, about three years ago.

Dan and Johnny were a little shorter than Bobby and a little younger, too. Dan had a shock of red hair, freckles, and a feisty disposition. Johnny had blond hair and still sported some baby fat. These two had lived next to each other all their lives. Dan's father taught history at Boston University and Johnny's father was a doctor.

"Okay. We've got a war to win!" said Bobby, bending over to pick up a couple of wooden rifles that were the key to their arsenal. "Come on. Baird, you bring the shovels, and, Johnny, get the pick-axe. Dan and I'll bring the war stuff."

"Stop being bossy," said Dan.

"Yeah, we haven't voted for a captain yet," said Johnny.

"Okay, anyone else want to be captain?" Bobby looked around the group. Dan stared back at him and started to say something but Baird spoke up first.

"Bobby should be captain," said Baird. "Pat's in the Marines and Mr. Swift was a sergeant. It runs in the family."

Dan grumbled, "You guys always stick up for each other." But didn't pursue the matter further.

"Okay, that's settled." Bobby took command. He sang out, "Fall in and forward march to the battlefield!" He swung his rifle in an arc toward the woods below the house. The soldiers shouldered their equipment and headed in ragged formation down the steep hill and into the woods.

The plan was to dig two parallel trenches about three feet deep and six feet long in the meadow on the far side of the woods, far from the prying eyes of parents. One would be for the Americans, the other, closer to the woods, for the Nazis. There would be about ten yards between the trenches for "no man's land." As the boys dug, they found the soil surprisingly soft, but it was a hot, hard job nevertheless. They pulled off their jerseys. As they worked in the strong June sun, sweat ran in shiny drops down their hairless white chests.

After a while, Dan threw down his shovel and said, "It's too hot to do this. Let's swim."

Bobby continued to dig furiously. "Are you kidding, Dan? We're just getting started."

"Come on, Dan, we'll never get finished if we goof off." said Baird.

"Anyway," said Johnny, "we don't have our suits and if we go in ballocky bare ass, we'll all see your peanuts, Baird"

Dan and Johnny laughed. When they had been wrestling recently, someone hit Baird accidentally in the crotch and he yelled, or so the others thought, "Oh, my peanuts." Bobby had started to laugh and stopped when he could see that Baird was embarrassed.

"Forget about that, will you." Baird changed the subject quickly. "Captain's right. We've got to go on for a while."

"Okay," said Dan. "Besides," and he started to giggle, "our nuts will shrivel when they hit the cold water."

That prospect kept them at their work for a while longer. However, they all finally got so hot and sweaty that Bobby said, "Okay, men, let's take a break." They stripped and rolled around in the nearby brook, yelling as the cold water hit their bodies.

"Let's see who can piss the farthest," said Dan.

"Not in the water," said Baird.

"Why not?" asked Dan as he sent a thin yellow arc a considerable distance down the brook where it quickly disappeared in the fast-moving water. "Beat that," he yelled in a high-pitched voice.

When they had finished the trenches, the boys uprooted the grass and flowers in between until there was nothing but scuffed-up dirt. To improve the fortifications, they put heaps of dirt along the top of each trench for machine gun emplacements and made piles of stones to be used for grenades.

"Okay, we got time for one mission before we head for the chow hall," said Bobby.

They decided on a sweep, the length of the meadow from the west to the trenches. No one responded to Captain Bobby's request for volunteers to be a German soldier, so he announced that, just this once, they would all charge together and simply pretend the Germans were there in the trench, resisting with full force. The Americans drew up in formation in the shadows at the west side of the meadow, a hundred yards away from the trench.

Baird tied a big red handkerchief to a long branch. "I'll be the flag bearer. He's the one the enemy shoots at first."

After some whispered last-minute instructions from Bobby and an artillery barrage to soften the enemy up, courtesy of Dan and Johnny, they were ready. With whoops and loud cries, they tore across the field, repeatedly dropping in the fragrant, sun-dappled grass, to fire their rifles at the foe. Each time they got up to continue the charge, they left outlines of their bodies in crushed daisies and grass.

Baird cried out once, "I'm hit!"

Bobby yelled, "No wounded today, Baird!"

When they reached the trenches, they jumped in and waved their rifles in the air in triumph. Baird jammed the flag into the ground in front of the trench to loud cheers.

Their baptism of fire over, the combatants piled their weapons beside the trenches and headed up the hill, pushing and shoving each other, ready for more but knowing it was time to get home.

"Okay," said Johnny. "This is great, huh? No more grown-ups near the trenches. We worked hard. This is our place. Right?"

They all nodded.

Just before they parted, Dan lifted his left leg and produced a prolonged fart. He smiled widely as the others groaned.

Bobby yelled, "Ah, they got me!"

Johnny shouted, "Gas attack! Gas attack!"

"Not as bad as your breath, buddy," said Dan, throwing his arm around Johnny.

Sunday morning at 10:30 the warriors were in the choir room, putting on their black robes and starched white collars. The final hateful touch to their dress was a fluffy black bowtie that had to be tied by the choir mother.

I can't wait until my voice changes so I can quit," Bobby said.

"You're getting close. I heard you cracking the other day," said Dan. "You're lucky."

"I'm glad the kids from Cochrane can't see us," said Johnny. "We look fruity."

Dan nodded his assent. "It's almost as bad as dancing school, wearing those stupid white gloves. Except we don't have to bow to weird Betty Ashton and stupid Mary Wood."

They thought Baird couldn't say anything negative because that would be disloyal to his father. The truth was, far from having negative feelings about being a choir boy in his father's church, Baird liked it very much. As he sat near God's altar, he would often imagine himself the minister of a congregation, leading them in prayer, preaching the good word and having the sacred honor of presiding over holy communion. He would be sorry when his voice changed and he had to sit in the congregation. It wouldn't be quite so easy to have these daydreams.

On this lovely June morning, the war seemed truly far away. As the hour of divine service approached, the parishioners filed into St. Christopher's, neighbor nodding to neighbor. They felt proud and lucky to worship in this lovely white clapboard church, built circa 1835. At 11 o'clock the first verse of "All things bright and beautiful" was heard faintly through the mahogany doors leading to the sacristy. The doors opened and the crucifer, carrying a plain silver cross, led the choir down the steps. Reverend C. Robert Jewell, singing loudly in his quavering bass, was at the end of the procession. Rev. Jewell was five foot seven inches and balding with just a fringe of graying hair. His face had a serious, rather pinched look, and he easily gained a five o'clock shadow. Born and raised in Birmingham, England, he used his bass voice and fine English accent to good effect in the reading of the gospels and prayers. But he did not do this to the point of affectation. The congregation knew him as a decent man. His wife, Edna, who was raised as a Quaker, had died a year ago of cancer.

Rev. Jewell's sermon was about finding God in nature and in the glories of a fine June day. The sunlight poured into the church, surrounding and supporting Rev. Jewell's message as he spoke. He ended at about 11:40, saying, "I am deliberately keeping my sermon this morning short so that you may be quicker to go outside and breathe in God's magic yourself.

And please remember that I have given you brevity this morning when you think I may go on too long on some winter Sunday."

The congregation chuckled.

As the choir filed out, singing the recessional, it occurred to Baird that he should offer to act as chaplain for their own small army. He would mention it to Bobby first thing on Monday.

When he got home from church, Patrick Swift felt irritated rather than refreshed. Funny, he thought, going to church didn't make him feel better. He had decided it had something to do with the many Yankees who were long-time members of the congregation. He felt they looked down on him.

Patrick made a lunch of peanut-butter-and-marshmallow sandwiches for Bobby and himself in their small kitchen, and they ate at the kitchen table. They each had an apple for dessert. Patrick looked at the pile of dirty dishes in the sink and the dust balls gathering in the corners of the room. Margaret had been sick for over a week. He thought he'd better do something about the mess in the kitchen.

After lunch he took a plate of food up to Margaret. She had been eating very little. The plain curtains in the bedroom were partly drawn, and the windows were closed. The only light in the room came from a lamp on the bedside table. Margaret was in bed, propped up on pillows. She looked haggard. Her hair had gotten so much grayer in the last year, Patrick thought. He looked at her picture on the bureau, taken shortly after they were married. Beautiful with long black hair and a face full of love and joy.

He handed her the plate. "Bob Jewell offered to come for a visit, but I told him you were in good hands. He said he misses seeing you in church every day."

"Well, I miss being there, but I don't want him coming here right now."

"He said he was sorry Edna wasn't still alive, because she could help you."

"I learned a lot from her actually, but I'm not sure she could help things right now. This is something I have to deal with myself." She sighed and sank a little lower on the pillows.

Something about this gesture irritated Patrick. How sick was she really? he wondered. "You know, I could never see what you liked about her. She talked too much. About peace and how great the Quakers were. Kind of high and mighty if you ask me. Why'd she marry an Episcopalian minister anyway?"

"She was a very decent woman."

"Do you really get that much out of going to church? You barely went after we were first married." Patrick couldn't let up on this point. "Now if you're not here, I know where to find you."

"Patrick, that's not funny. We do what we have to do." Then, she sat up in bed. "I'm going to come downstairs and sweep up a little this afternoon."

"Margaret, that's silly. You're sick. Stay in bed. I'll take care of it."

"I'll bet nothing much has been done down there lately."

"Margaret, I said I'll take care of it." Patrick was getting angry. "Look, I'm going down and read the Herald."

While Patrick tried to read the Sunday paper, Bobby was hanging around him, pretending to be playing.

"Bobby, what do you want? You're bothering me. Why don't you go out and play."

"Dad, I'm worried about Mom. Please tell me what's really up. She's been sick for a week already."

Patrick, with a sigh, put the paper down. "Dr. Fayerweather says she'll be all right. She has to take it easy for a few days. If she doesn't feel better, he'll do some tests."

He looked at Bobby and could see he was upset. "Bobby, she'll be all right," he said in a louder voice, trying to be reassuring.

Bobby pressed on with his concerns. "What about Pat? She's really worried about him, isn't she? He's going to be fighting soon, right? Yeah, I'm sure that's part of it."

His father indicated with a gesture of his hand he didn't think his wife should be so worried. "The way I see it, Pat's off doing what he has to do for his country. I'm proud of him." He picked up the paper again and turned from the sports section to the comics. "Let's change the subject, huh? How's it going in the trenches?"

"Well, they made me captain. I think a lot of it is because you were in the Army and Pat's in the Marines."

"That's fair. Good experience to lead." He put the paper down and his voice brightened. "Whip them into shape. That's what you've got to do."

"Actually," said Bobby. "I sort of took the job over without being asked, but then Baird said I should do it because of Pat and you."

"Don't let that Munroe kid get superior on you. His father thinks he's big stuff, teaching at BU. You know the old saying, don't you? Those who can do. Those who can't teach." He chuckled to himself. "Or that Johnny either, although I have to say Willard Fayerweather seems to be a pretty straight guy."

"Dad, these guys are my friends. I think they're great! And Baird's my best friend, you know."

"Yeah, Baird seems like a pretty smart kid. I've watched him up in the choir stall. I think he really likes the churchy stuff. Maybe he'll be a preacher, too, like his old man. Maybe, go him one better." He laughed. "Hey, forget I said that." He paused. "You know what I'd really like? I wish I were younger and could go fight. Fighting's sure better than being a damn insurance salesman."

"I miss Pat a lot. Maybe I'll join like the two of you someday." Bobby said, because he figured it was the right thing to say.

"Remember this, Bobby." Patrick pointed at Bobby, wagging his finger up and down to emphasize the point. "The only way that people will really respect you is if you are strong and fight for your beliefs. People are always trying to take something away from you. That's a hard message, son, but it's the way life is."

Patrick reached over and put his hand on Bobby's shoulder. Bobby couldn't remember the last time his father had done that.

Bobby nodded, "I think I understand, Dad."

Rev. Jewell and Baird sat at opposite ends of the polished mahogany table in the dining room while Mrs. Page served a meal of roast beef with Yorkshire pudding and roast potatoes. The menu for Sunday dinner never changed. It was as regular as the order of the church service just concluded.

His father preferred that Baird not initiate subjects at Sunday dinner, so nothing was said until Rev. Jewell cleared his throat and asked, "How is it going with your playmates? You told me you were going to do something down in the Munroes' meadow that you were excited about? I'm sorry. I can't remember the details. Tell me about it."

Baird wondered if his father really wanted to know what was going on. It was hard work talking to his father, and mostly he got suggestions about what he ought to be doing to lead a more Christian life. Sunday dinner had been a special and happy occasion when his mother was alive. She always made sure there was good conversation and laughter during the meal. Now often little was said. Baird had decided this was because his father was preoccupied. The church service had just ended, and he was still in some way close to God.

"Well, we have dug some trenches down in Munroes' meadow, and we're going to play Americans and Germans fighting. Bobby's the captain because Pat's in the Marines and Mr. Swift was a sergeant in the Army."

His father interrupted, "Baird, I know that about Pat and Patrick Swift."

"Yes, Daddy."

"Baird, please call me 'Father' and not 'Daddy.' You're more than twelve years old now, right?"

"Yes, Father." Baird didn't feel like talking much more, but he did have one thing on his mind, and wanted to know what his father thought. "Do you mind that we're playing war and all?"

"Well, Baird, you know what your mother thought about war, and I am beginning to think more and more that she was right." He, too, wished that Edna was with them. He knew he was being a little stiff and tried to lighten up. "But you're young and you're playing. It's really a game, I think, like playing baseball or football." He thought about his analogy. "Yes, I don't really see the difference. It's just a game." He looked sternly at Baird. "Just don't take it all too seriously."

"Okay, I won't," said Baird. "I'm going to volunteer to be the chaplain for our group." He thought his father would be pleased at that.

His father smiled in a way Baird couldn't quite understand, but he thought perhaps his father was laughing at him for having such a grand thought.

"Son, I'm not sure that's part of playing. Being a chaplain, being a minister, is not a game. You need training and have to have a calling. You have to be humble." He nodded to emphasize his agreement with that thought. "Yes, you have to be humble," he said again.

Baird thought his father was going to forbid him to be the chaplain. But Rev. Jewell went on to say, "Son, I think that it's all right to be the chaplain, if you do it knowing in all humility that you are not really a minister. It could help you understand what it's like to have that responsibility." He found other reasons not to disapprove. "I suppose being a chaplain is no different than being a medic. It's a part of every Army unit, isn't it?"

Baird wasn't sure about everything his father was saying but he decided he wasn't saying no.

"I've thought about being the medic, too."

"That's fine, Baird, fine," his father said as he rang the bell for Mrs. Page to clear the table and bring in the vanilla ice cream with butterscotch sauce. Baird ate his portion, not nearly as much as he would have liked. Nobody offered him seconds. He left the table with a feeling that made him uncomfortable. He believed very much in God and wanted to do the right thing. But he wondered if he really had to work so hard to be good. A lot of the things he did to try to please didn't seem to work out so well.

The boys were back in the trenches early on Monday morning with the weather growing hotter.

"Look," said Bobby. "Two guys have to be the enemy here. Baird, you be a German, okay?"

"Okay, I will today. But I have been thinking. Maybe I could act as our chaplain. You know, provide spiritual guidance and pray over the dying and wounded. That sort of stuff."

Bobby said, "Well, I would like my company to have a chaplain, and a medic, too, for that matter, but I can't spare you from the fighting, Baird."

Baird was about to say, "I want to be the medic, too," but Bobby had already looked over at Dan and Johnny.

"Okay, who else volunteers?"

"Bobby, why don't you pick yourself as the other German?" said Johnny.

"I'm the captain," he declared loudly. Then, he looked down at the ground and said in a low voice, "I sort of can't do it today. I'll tell you later."

"All right, let's stop messing around here," Dan said. "I'll be the other damn German." He accepted his assignment for the day by giving a Nazi salute to Bobby. "Yahwol, mein kommandant."

Combat began in earnest. The rules of warfare were developed quickly. The Nazis would occupy the trench nearest the grove, while the Americans, after an artillery barrage to soften the enemy up, would charge across the meadow and jump into their trench. There would be an exchange of heavy fire and the hurling of grenades before the final assault by the Americans. It was understood that the Americans would win every battle, although the Germans were allowed an occasional counterattack. The Germans would always be shot and die painfully, dropping their rifles and clutching their hearts as they fell in the dirt. Surrender was not permitted because of a shortage of soldiers.

Baird was torn between the need for appropriate humility and the really strong desire to act as the chaplain. From time to time, he would pretend to himself that he was on his knees administering to a fallen soldier and had to resist the urge to do it. Once he actually did drop to his knees to minister to Dan who was wounded and dying, but Bobby gave him a hard stare and Dan pushed him away.

A few days into the serious combat, when everyone but Bobby had taken a turn as a German, the others wanted to know what was going on.

"Fair's fair, Bobby. What's going on here?" Dan asked.

Bobby looked down and shuffled his feet in the dirt and said, "Aw, come on. I just can't be a German."

"What do you mean you can't be a German?" said Johnny.

Bobby spoke so softly they could barely hear him. "My Dad wouldn't like it if I were a Nazi. He calls them fascist pigs. He'd think it wasn't fair to Pat. Dad's getting really worked up about fighting in the war. He says he wishes he were young enough to fight!"

"Look, he's not going to find out," said Dan. "He's not going to spy on us. You just can't be the good guy all the time."

Baird thought a little. "How about this? You only have to be the enemy half as much as the rest of us. What do you think, guys? Look, Bobby, we're all swearing that we won't tell our parents."

The others raised their right hands and nodded. Bobby shrugged a reluctant consent.

"Now can we play? Hey, we're pals. Let's have some fun," said Johnny.

On Saturday, July 21, a letter arrived from Pat indicating that he was heading not toward Europe, as the family had assumed, but to an unknown destination in the Pacific. He said he loved his family and told them all not to worry. Margaret sat in a chair by the window in her bedroom, reading and rereading Pat's letter. She knew that it was time for her to get up and get moving. She couldn't hope any longer for a miracle, like her son sustaining some minor injury, just serious enough so he would be discharged and sent home. That had been weakness, and there was no more time for weakness, not that there ever was.

The following Monday morning, when Bobby came down to breakfast, his mother was in the kitchen making scrambled eggs and bacon for his breakfast.

"When you're finished," she said, "I'm going to get after this kitchen floor."

"Gee, glad you're feeling better," Bobby said. They hugged and he sat down at the table. He thought she still looked pretty weak and pale.

"You were sick a long time."

"I'm feeling a lot better, and I'm tough. Anyway, I got sick of lying around. This house would fall apart if I didn't get up. " She turned from the stove with his plate, put it down in front of him and sat down. "I bet you've missed your mom's cooking."

Bobby nodded his head several times. "You bet I have."

"Your father told you that we have a letter from Pat that he's on his way to the Pacific." Margaret tried to keep her voice steady.

"Yeah, he said that the letter was delayed or something, so he might be there pretty soon."

"We'll all have to pray for him. Promise me you will."

"Of course I will, Mom."

Margaret bent over Bobby and patted the top of his head. "I'm sorry that I haven't really been able to talk to you seriously much for a while. Have you been a good boy?"

"Yeah, I think so."

"You mentioned something about playing out behind the Munroes'. I'm afraid I didn't catch too much of that." Margaret walked back to the stove to clean up a bit.

"Well, we've dug some trenches down behind Munroes' and are playing there."

"Playing what?"

"Playing, like, Americans and Germans and that stuff." He could see where the conversation was heading and added, "Mrs. Fayerweather's been taking us swimming too. It's fun."

"You're playing war, aren't you?" Her voice rose to a mildly accusatory pitch. "I really wish you wouldn't do that. It upsets me."

"Mom, we're just playing, and they made me captain. Dad thought it was great."

"I'm sure." She rolled her eyes. "Well, it upsets me. I don't like war."

"Were you sick because of Pat?"

"Bobby, just finish your breakfast and let me clean here." She paused and went on. "I was sick because I was sick." She looked at him and softened a bit. "Of course I'm worried about my son being in the Marines. But I can't help him lying around."

"I'm going to play with the boys. Please don't be upset. I think maybe I'm helping Pat somehow."

"How could you do that?"

"I don't know really. It's just a feeling."

"I'm going to church after I do a few things around the house. I'll leave your lunch."

"I'll see you later, Mom. I'm trying to pray for Pat, too." He wanted to give her a hug before leaving but she was already headed for the closet to get a broom. "I'm really glad you're feeling better," he said as he went out the door.

Patrick had assumed without question that his son would be fighting the Germans, the chance he had missed in World War I. Now he had to change his view quickly. That same night after supper Patrick Swift took Bobby out to the front porch and talked to him directly and sternly about the Japanese whom Pat would be fighting. About how cruel they were and how they tortured their prisoners in horrible ways. They're much worse than the Germans, Patrick told him in a voice that became so loud Margaret came out and told him to quiet down and to stop telling his son such evil things.

It rained so hard Tuesday the boys didn't play together. On Wednesday the sun came out and the boys met at the trenches. Bobby was there when Dan and Johnny arrived, but he barely acknowledged their presence. When Baird came around the corner a minute later, Bobby took charge immediately, yelling at his troops. "One thing we got to get straight right away: Pat's in the Pacific. He's going to be fighting the Japs." He spat the word out. "My father says I can't ever be a Jap. That's disloyal to Pat. I promised

I wouldn't be." He picked up his rifle and pumped it in the air. "My father says they're yellow bastards—that's what he says they are! We're only going to kill Japs from now on!" He pumped the rifle up and down a few more times and said in a rough voice, "We've got to beat those yellow bastards."

There was a long pause. No one was prepared to countermand Bobby's orders about the change of enemy. But Baird broke the silence on another point.

"Bobby, I'm sorry, but that's not a nice thing to say. They're Japanese people, not Japs or yellow—that word."

Bobby raised his voice. "Yellow bastards, yellow bastards, yellow bastards! Hey, my brother's over there. If they capture him they'll do horrible things to him."

Baird looked as if Bobby had punched him.

"Hey, take it easy, Bobby," said Dan.

"Wait a minute. Hold on," said Johnny. "Let's get this organized. Pat's over there getting ready to fight. We've got to help him."

"Okay, okay," said Baird. "I was wrong." He remembered the need to be humble. "I guess Bobby can say yellow b…that word, as much as he wants if it makes him feel better. And I'll be a Japanese soldier all the time so Bobby doesn't have to do it."

A quick look of relief passed over Bobby's face. Then, he quickly became stern again. "The Japs are really mean bastards. We've got to be tough, too."

Later Baird thought to himself, Did I really have to back off like that and do what Bobby wanted? He didn't hesitate too long. His brother's at real war. He's my best friend. I've got to be extra nice to him.

Rev. Jewell sat in the mahogany-paneled study in the rectory, reworking his sermon for the coming Sunday, August 20. The sun was setting, and he could see out the window the steeple of St. Christopher's catching the last rays of sunlight. The rest of the church was shrouded in darkness, so the steeple seemed to be floating, detached from all support. But the church was always there, he thought, whether seen or not. He glanced over the lines he had just written. He knew what a dramatic impact his words would have. Was he really the same person who had, as a young clergyman, felt that war might be a sometimes unfortunate necessity in order to spread Christianity and Western civilization around the globe?

Rev. Jewell knew much of his change of heart was the result of Edna's influence. He appreciated her hatred of war more as time went by. He would acknowledge her contribution to his thinking. He loved and missed his wife so much. He hoped his words would be a memorial to her as well.

The timing, he realized, might be problematic. Just two days ago the Swifts had received word that Pat was missing in action after he and his fellow Marines had battled the Japanese for a vital air strip in the Solomon Islands on August 7 and 8. Margaret had visited him after the news had come about Pat. He had been surprised and proud at how strong and steady she was. She's found great strength somehow in her tragedy, he thought.

But should he wait in deference to the Swifts and their most unfortunate situation? After some deliberation, he said to himself if this is the right thing, it must transcend personal considerations. If there were no war, Pat would be with his family now. He picked up his pen and continued writing.

On Sunday, as always, the crucifer, choir, and Rev. Jewell emerged from the Sacristy, proceeded down the aisles, and headed toward the altar. But, as the service progressed, seasoned parishioners noticed he didn't linger as lovingly as usual over the prayers and gospels. And when he ascended to the pulpit, a look of nervous determination had replaced his usual benevolent smile.

"My dear parishioners," he began, "the war has truly come home to Newton. One of our parishioners, Patrick Swift, Jr., has been reported missing in action. Our hearts and prayers go out to the Swifts—Patrick and Margaret and young Bobby. We pray to God that Pat will come home safe and sound to his family and his church very soon. Other sons of St. Christopher have enlisted in our fighting forces and will soon be engaged in this great worldwide conflict.

"As the war begins to touch our St. Christopher family directly, I have been struggling for the grace to determine God's will in the matter of war. I have not had my dear Edna's sage advice. But since she died, her Quaker principles have loomed larger and larger in my thinking. Many of you may disagree with what I am about to say or misunderstand my motives, but I hope that you will think hard on my message and know that it is my best effort to interpret God's word."

He looked in the direction of the Swifts before resuming. "You all know that we are engaged in a bloody war where young men of almost every nation are being forced to kill their fellow man in the name of some ideal. In the Allies' case, we are killing in the name of freedom and democracy.

"'Yes,' you will say, 'we know war is horrible. We are not a warlike people. But what choice had we? We were attacked early on a Sunday morning by the Japanese. The Nazis occupy most of Europe and have persecuted the Jews and others as part of their rise to power. What choice had we but to defend with our blood, our precious way of life?'"

Not a head in the congregation nodded in sleep. What was coming? A haggard Patrick Swift frowned and twisted in his pew. Margaret was beside him this morning, looking pale but composed.

"But war itself is wrong. Even the most righteous, when they go to war, lose their righteousness and soon have hatred and vengeance in their hearts. They become no better than the enemy, seeking an eye for an eye, determined to win at any cost. Thus, we, the Allies, doing our best to overcome the other side with superior weight of men and machine, are, in a sense, no better than the Germans and the Japanese! We are defending the institution of war."

Patrick Swift's face was now dark red. He clenched and unclenched his large fists. There was so much movement and whispering in the Church that Rev. Jewell, despite the intensity of his delivery, could not easily be heard.

He moved on to his conclusion. "My dear parishioners, I am not a naïve man. I know the realities of our world. I know the war will continue. What I ask is that you individually search your hearts and try to hear an inner voice, which will be Christ's voice, telling you that war only breeds hatred and more hatred and war, followed by more war. War—- everlasting war. I ask you to listen carefully to that voice and, after hearing it, take whatever action you can to promote true peace in the world. Ultimately, only a refusal to fight—only taking as our guide the words of our Lord when he said to turn the other cheek will bring peace on earth. There is never a perfect time to start. The time is now."

Patrick Swift had had enough. He rose to his feet, beckoned to Margaret, and then tugged on her arm to get her to follow him. She pulled her arm away and didn't get up. He glared at her and marched, head held high, down the aisle and out the church door. Bobby, sitting in the choir stall, looked away, embarrassed.

As always, Rev. Jewell stood at the back of the church to greet parishioners. This Sunday, a number hurried by him, believing he had in fact gone too far, but a considerable number, including the Munroes and Fayerweathers, shook his hand. A few because they agreed with his message, no doubt, but, whatever they believed, most wanted to preserve the longstanding tradition of collegiality at St. Christopher's.

When the last of the congregation had left, Rev. Jewell was heading back to the sacristy when he sensed someone entering the church. As he turned, Patrick Swift approached, flushed and angry. Margaret was behind him, trying to restrain him and saying, "Patrick, Patrick, please calm down. Get control of yourself. Come home with me." Rev. Jewell drew himself up and waited calmly as Patrick Swift approached. No one noticed Bobby and Baird, who had come into the church separately and were standing in the back.

Patrick stopped just in front of the minister. "Jewell, you hypocrite, what the hell has gotten into you? My son is missing in action. You've got the nerve to come out with all this crap. I don't want you praying for Pat." His voice rose. "Jesus, what kind of enemy propaganda are you dishing out in God's name here? America is wrong? The Allies are evil? You should be ashamed of yourself when our boys are fighting and dying."

Patrick stopped, breathless with anger. Margaret said as calmly as she could, "Come along now, Patrick. That's enough." She took his arm and tried to lead him away. "He's so upset about Pat," she offered to Rev. Jewell.

But Patrick wasn't finished. He shrugged off his wife's hand roughly and moved even closer to Rev. Jewell, who had clasped his hands in front of him.

"Patrick," said Rev. Jewell, "I had hoped we could talk about this. You, of all people, I want to understand my position and how difficult it is. But I do believe it is God's way. I am truly sorry about your son. I understand how you must feel. Please believe me!"

He tried to put his hand on Patrick's shoulder, but Patrick brushed it off angrily.

He said, "There's nothing to talk about until you say God is on our side and Patrick's not dying for an evil cause. Maybe, not even then. We're finished here at St. Christopher's. How can you call yourself a man of God?" His whole body shook. He was on the verge of losing control and striking Rev. Jewell.

Margaret stepped between them. "Patrick, just stop it," she said firmly. Finally, Patrick stepped back, glaring at the minister. Then he turned and lurched down the aisle and out the side door of St Christopher's.

Patrick arrived home at two o'clock in a very dark mood. Margaret had been crying when she got home earlier, but now she was waiting on the porch and followed him into the house, determined to have it out with her husband. "Patrick, what got into you? Yelling at Rev. Jewell isn't going to bring Pat back. If it wasn't for the war, we'd all be together right now. Rev. Jewell is right! War is bad."

"Margaret, don't start on me." He held up his hands to emphasize the point. "Just cut it out. Why didn't you back me up against that hypocrite? What kind of wife are you?"

"Don't say that to me, Patrick," she shot back. "I'm a wife trying to help a husband who's on the verge of disgracing himself and his family."

"Look, I'm not going back to that church until he says he was wrong. Wrong! Wrong! Wrong! Christ, I can't believe we were friends once. God doesn't want us to lie down and roll over so the goddamn Nazis and Japs can win the war. For Chrissake!" He began stomping back and forth across the living room.

"Please, please, Patrick. Stop taking the Lord's name in vain. Rev. Jewell's saying what he believes. We've got to pray for our son. We have to go to the church to pray. Otherwise we're not doing everything we can to help him."

"Goddamn it! You let me down, not leaving the church with me. You're taking his side in this."

He walked toward her menacingly, but Margaret stood her ground and he abruptly stopped. She shook her head sadly, tears in her eyes.

"All I want is to get my son back."

Patrick yelled, "Get in here, Bobby, right now. Hurry up. Move!" Bobby was in the living room quickly.

"Your mother says we need to pray for Pat. I agree with your mother." Patrick's voice was quiet but had a cold edge. "We're going to pray right here, right now." Patrick went down, heavily, to his knees.

Bobby gave a worried look in his mother's direction and started to kneel. His mother remained standing, so he stopped, halfway down, in an awkward crouch.

Margaret said, "Patrick, this is not right. You've got to clear your heart first. God won't listen to you in this state." She turned and went into the next room. Bobby remained in his crouch.

"God," roared Patrick. "We know you are on America's side. I know you'll help us beat the Axis. Make America a mighty fist, oh, God, to hammer the enemies of freedom. We have given you our son to fight this great fight. Please bring him back to us, but if he is dead, make it not in vain. Help us defeat those who killed him and do it in your name. Amen."

"There!" Patrick grunted his way back on his feet and, glaring in Margaret's direction, left the house. Bobby rose from his crouch and went to a chair, where he slumped. Margaret came into the room, stood behind his chair and put her hands on his shoulders.

"I'm sorry you had to hear all that. We should pray together for your brother and your father."

Bobby shrugged off his mother's hands and looked down at the floor. He didn't want to take sides. His mother had more to say to him. She came around in front of the chair, put her hand under his chin, and raised his head up so she could look directly into his eyes.

"Bobby, this may not be the best time to say this, but I don't think I have a choice. I can't do much about your father, but you're different." He tried to look away but she held his gaze. "I want you to stop going to the trenches and doing that horrible war thing. Think of your brother. How can you be fighting when we don't know where he is, whether he's alive or not?"

"I don't know. I don't know." Bobby was crying. What was he supposed to do? He was being pulled in all directions. "I don't think I can. I think I'm helping Pat. Almost keeping him alive by doing it." He got to his feet and yelled at his mother. "Why do we fight all the time when we should all be together to help Pat?"

His mother looked so sad after he yelled that he gave her a hug and said, "I'm sorry. I'm sorry. I'm trying to pray and I can't. I'm too angry. I just think as long as I'm fighting that Pat is alive and fighting, too."

Then Bobby turned and ran out the door.

After he watched Patrick Swift storm out of church, Baird wondered what he could do now to help his friend. Bobby's mother was after him to pray all the time for Pat. She hated that he was playing war games. And it had been pretty obvious Patrick Swift thought it was great Pat was fighting and Bobby should fight hard in the trenches. Now the situation was even more complicated after the bad news about Pat, the sermon, and the terrible scene in church. As far as Baird could see, Bobby was coming down on his father's side, wanting to fight all the time. He didn't think he was praying very much.

He wondered now if Bobby would even talk to him or if Bobby's father would let him play anymore. Baird knew his father hadn't meant to make Patrick Swift angry. But he wondered if it was really right to bring up that whole big question about war the very Sunday after his family found out Pat was missing.

His father had retreated to his study right after dinner, at which not a word was said about the sermon or Patrick Swift. Baird was sure his father didn't know he was in church and had seen and heard the whole argument. If only he could discuss these things with him. He also wanted to talk to his father about Bobby, but this wasn't a good time. As he sat there, wondering what to do, he had more of the thoughts he had been having lately about trying too hard to please people because that was the right thing to do. If he was going to help his friend out, he was going to have to figure out something on his own and take action. He felt himself getting ready to stand on his own two feet. Be humble. Bobby was taking action. Mr. Swift was too. Even his father was. Why not him?

Everyone showed at the trenches on Monday. Nothing was said about church or any problem after church. Fall was in the air. School would be starting in a few days. Queen Anne's lace and goldenrod had replaced the daisies in the few portions of the Munroe meadow not ravaged by the summer warfare. While nothing was said about Sunday or the fact that Pat was missing, it was immediately clear that the war down the hill from the Munroes' house had entered a new phase. The shoving, the pushing and jostling, the farting games, the fun which had been a big part of the early war phase and which had been diminishing in frequency anyway as the summer went on now ceased completely.

There was just killing and more killing, and there was a new quality brought to the killing by Bobby. He had a wooden bayonet on his rifle all the time and used it exclusively to finish off the hated Japanese. Bobby would thrust and stab at Baird with his fixed bayonet, yelling at the top of his lungs "Take that you yellow bastard," or "That's for my brother!" Baird never flinched or complained. He took the role of Japanese soldier seriously. He put up such a tough fight at times that Bobby was hard put to make the final kill. Sometimes, before stoically accepting the inevitable end, Baird would fight so hard and well that Bobby could tell that Baird had become much stronger over the course of the summer.

A few days after the new phase of combat started, Bobby headed home on the run just after the day's battle had ended. Baird ran after him, yelling, "Wait up, Bobby. I want to talk to you."

"What do you want to talk about?"

Bobby was still flushed and angry after the afternoon's heavy fighting and kept on moving.

"Look, I'm still your friend, your best friend. You know that," said Baird, running along beside him.

Bobby grunted.

"Hey, what's going on? You're just getting madder all the time."

"So what? The Japs got my brother. I got to do this."

"Well, I don't like it. I feel like you hate me. Like you hate everybody almost."

"No, No," said Bobby, sounding like he didn't really care or mean it. "I only hate the Japs."

"Bobby," Baird said, "I've been thinking a lot about this, and I've got some ideas."

"Leave me alone, will you!"

Bobby tried to get away, but Baird came around in front of him and blocked his way.

"Just stop!" Baird said sharply.

Bobby looked at Baird, who looked like he was ready for a fight. Bobby wasn't prepared for that. He shrugged.

"Okay, what kind of ideas?"

"Do you remember when I said I could be the chaplain for the group and you wouldn't let me?

"Yeah."

"Okay, so I went along with that. Now I'm going along with being a Japanese soldier and letting you beat the shit out of me." Bobby's head jerked up in surprise at Baird's first use of the word. "I don't have to do that. I've been doing it to make you feel better about your brother, and it's not working. I was wrong."

"Baird, I don't know what you're talking about!"

"Yes, you do, Bobby. Look, this is crazy, what's going on. Dan and Johnny hate it. It's not making anybody feel good. If we're going to keep this up, I'm not going to be the Japanese soldier all the time and I'm going to be the chaplain. We need that. There's too much hate around. Plus, no more screaming out you-know-what. Otherwise I'm quitting."

"You sound like your goddamn father."

"Cut it out, Bobby," said Baird. "I'm not my father."

Bobby said more quietly, "Baird, you can't quit."

"Why not? Sure I can."

Bobby didn't try to answer that one. He didn't have to. Baird knew that Bobby needed to fight him, not one of the others.

The two faced each other. "What's it going to be?" said Baird. Then, he went on. "Maybe there's another way. I'll give you another choice," said Baird. "We'll fight. If I win, then you do what I say. If not, we'll keep on the same way."

Now Bobby felt like he had to calm Baird down.

"Jesus, Baird, what's happening to you? Look, I don't know. Let me alone, okay."

He thought for a second or two.

"What do you want me to do?"

"I want us to pray together to stop the hate."

"You're kidding." Bobby gave a strained laugh. "Now you really sound like your old man."

"Hey, you got a choice. Just let me know what you want to do before we start tomorrow."

The next day, August 29, was cold, with a northeast wind and a light rain. The trenches were filled with mud and cold, dirty water. The boys assembled, ready to play for a while.

Bobby announced to the troops, "Baird is going to be the only Japanese soldier, and the rest of us will be Americans. Then, we'll charge and just see what happens after that."

"Nothing new about that. That's fine with me," said Dan. "Who wants to be a Jap anyway?"

Baird ignored the provocation and hunkered down in the trench, while the three Americans started the assault. They wriggled through the grass toward the trench, softening the enemy with the usual procedures. There was no resistance or sound of any kind. As the Americans began the final charge, bayonets at the ready, they saw a white flag appear. Then, Baird stood up and threw down his rifle and stepped out of the trench, hands in the air. He bowed and said, "I surrender to you, honorable Captain Swift. I insist on terms of Geneva Conventions."

Bobby walked up to Baird. "Okay, you're my prisoner. Don't try anything funny."

He turned to Dan and Johnny. "I'll be responsible for the prisoner. I am going to take him to the stockade for questioning."

Dan said, "Why not do it here? I might have a few questions for the prisoner." He giggled. "I'd like to hear his Japanese accent again."

"No, soldier. This is my prisoner. The interrogation has to be one on one to be effective. I'm taking him to the stockade. You stay here and guard against a counterattack."

"Bullshit," said Dan.

"Obey orders, soldier. You have a valuable role to play here."

"We're not just going to stand around in the rain. Maybe we'll just take off. Right, Johnny?"

"Suit yourself, soldier. But there may be court martial proceedings here." Bobby remained calm in the face of Dan's provocation.

Baird put his hands on his head and walked in front of Bobby. Baird's pants were soaking wet from squatting in the trench, and he was shivering. The rain was falling harder now.

When they got out of sight in the grove, Baird put his hands down and took charge. "Okay, that was good. I'll take over."

Bobby shrugged. "This is pretty weird, Baird. I don't know why I'm doing it."

"Yes, you do," said Baird in a quiet voice. "We do this or I won't play anymore."

They walked toward a clearing in the middle of the grove. The trees were bending in the wind and the first leaves were being torn from the branches and falling around them. When they got to the clearing, Baird went to a bush and pulled out one of the black choir cassocks he had hidden earlier. He put it on, wet as it was. Then, he took a prayer book and a piece of paper out of his pocket and handed Bobby the paper. "Here, you read from this. I'll tell you when it's your turn."

He walked to the center of the clearing, tipped his head back and raised both arms high toward an opening in the trees with a supplicating gesture like his father. Then, he turned solemnly to Bobby, who was standing at the edge of the clearing, and said quietly, "Swift, have you anything to say to me?"

Bobby looked around, desperate to escape, but finally looked at the paper and read.

"Yes, Jewell, I have. I hate what you have said about the war and the goodness of our enemies." He looked at Baird and said, "What is this? I can't read your scribble."

"You're doing fine. Go on."

"I despise it and feel you are disloyal to my son, Pat who is serving his country so valiantly." Bobby had to struggle over some of the phrases but kept going. "I'm never coming to your church again. What do you say to that?"

He put the paper down. "Baird, what kind of crap is this? I'm getting out of here."

"Stay where you are," commanded Baird. Then, he raised his hand and made the sign of the cross. "Swift, I absolve and forgive you, understanding your grief and the grief of your family, which I underestimated. I, in turn, ask your forgiveness. I was wrong to preach that sermon when you just heard about your son's capture. I ask you humbly to come back to St. Christopher's. Now please join me in prayer for the safe return of Patrick, Jr." He, too, was looking at a sheet of paper in his hand. "Kneel with me, Swift." Baird knelt and waited. Bobby was not kneeling. Baird looked at him hard and started to get up. Bobby reluctantly sank to his knees.

Baird began to read. "Heavenly father, we, your humble and un-worthy servants, not fit to gather up the crumbs under thy table, humbly beseech you to spare thy servant Patrick Swift, Jr., and keep him safe from all harm. We are sure through your grace he is alive and well. Protect him, oh, Lord, and bring him back to his family and loved ones. And bring peace and understanding to all, both here in Newton and everywhere in the world. Make our allies and our enemies understand the error of their ways so that the world may be spared more deaths and agonies. And comfort the parents and brothers and sisters of those who serve and are missing and particularly thy servants Patrick and Margaret Swift and their second son Robert Regan Swift. In thy name we ask it. Amen."

"Can we quit now?" said Bobby. He looked wet and miserable.

"Say amen, Swift," commanded Baird.

"A-men!" Bobby finally said, after a long pause.

They both stood.

"All right," said Bobby, "Are we through, Baird? Let's go fight."

"Yeah, but remember, no more screaming. If it happens again, I quit. And I'm the chaplain, right?"

Bobby gave a small nod. "We should have fought, like you said. Then, I wouldn't have had to do this."

"Don't be too sure," said Baird.

Bobby shrugged. "Go back to the trenches. I'll be there in a few minutes."

"Okay."

Baird trudged through the wet woods and out into the meadow. Dan and Johnny were nowhere to be seen. He lowered himself into the cold slop of the American trench and waited for what seemed like forever. He was shiv-ering with the cold and wet. He felt a little silly and knew he hadn't been very humble but, all in all, he figured he had done the right thing. Rain continued to pour down, and it had become very dark even though it was only about 5:30 in the afternoon.

Finally, Baird could see Bobby coming toward him. When he got to the trench, Bobby paused at the edge. Baird noticed that Bobby had tears in his eyes and waited for him to speak. Finally, Bobby said, "You know, I'm sure my brother's dead by now. This whole thing is stupid—what you did, what I've been doing. He's dead."

Baird stood up and held out his hand to Bobby, who grabbed it and jumped into the trench. He squatted down next to Baird, and they just sat there in the cold watery trench, not talking, while the rain poured down and the early darkness thickened toward night. After a while, Baird put his arm around Bobby and said, "School starts next Tuesday."